Murder Before Dinner . . .

"Pam, dear," the voice said. "This is Aunt Lucy. I—I guess we can't have dinner with you and Gerald. Oh, it's so dreadful. You see, Thelma—"

"Aunt Lucy!" Pam said. "Something's happened? To Aunt Thelma?"

"Not yet," Lucinda said. "At least, I don't think so. I'm downstairs telephoning. They said it would be all right, but there's—I think there's one of them out there."

"Aunt Lucy!" Pam said. "What—"

"But they're so suspicious," Aunt Lucinda said. "And anyway, I don't think any of us could eat. It's all—all so dreadful!" The light, suddenly old, voice broke.

"Dear," Pam said. "Tell me. What's happened to Aunt Thelma."

"They—they're going to— Oh, *Pam!*"

Pamela North waited.

"—arrest her," Aunt Lucinda said. "It—it just can't be happening. It *can't* be!"

"Arrest her?" Pam said, her own voice rising. With her head she gestured to Jerry to get on the extension telephone in his study. He nodded, and went. "What on earth for?"

"Pamela," Aunt Lucinda said, "I'm afraid—dreadfully afraid—murder."

Books by Frances and Richard Lockridge

Murder Comes First
Murder Within Murder

Published by POCKET BOOKS

MURDER
COMES
FIRST

RICHARD AND
FRANCES LOCKRIDGE

PUBLISHED BY POCKET BOOKS NEW YORK

POCKET BOOKS, a Simon & Schuster division of
GULF & WESTERN CORPORATION
1230 Avenue of the Americas, New York, N.Y. 10020

Published by arrangement with J. B. Lippincott Company

ISBN: 0-671-44335-6

First Pocket Books printing July, 1982

10 9 8 7 6 5 4 3 2 1

POCKET and colophon are trademarks of Simon & Schuster.

Printed in the U.S.A.

MURDER
COMES
FIRST

1

It was a very fine morning. Little of it, to be sure, could get into the apartment in lower Manhattan of Mr. and Mrs. Gerald North—a thin wedge of the day's sunshine had forced a window and now lay on the floor, exhausted by its effort; through open windows there came a tentative freshness which was surely mid-October air, with the summer's humidity wrung out of it. The air had been a little over-used, was hand-me-down air, but there it was, almost breathable. Gerald North lowered his newspaper onto the breakfast table, gave the news he had read the reproachful sigh which was no more than its due, and breathed some of the air. He said it looked like being a nice weekend.

"Um," said Pam North, reading the mail. "Oh."

"The weather," Jerry said. "Nice out. I looked. Fair and continued warm through tomorrow." He lighted a cigarette and inhaled deeply. "Why don't we get the car and drive up to camp? Maybe stay overnight? Look at leaves?"

"Oh Jerry," Pam said. "The aunts."

"No worse than usual, I shouldn't think," Jerry North said. "Anyway, I wasn't suggesting a picnic."

Pam re-pronounced the word. She started to spell it.

"Listen," Jerry said, and ran the fingers of his right

7

hand through his hair. "Not Aunt Flora? The one with the wig?"

"They're in California," Pam said. She paused, and said she meant Aunt Flora and her new husband. "But the wig too, I guess," she added. "No, these are the Cleveland ones." She regarded her husband, who did not look enlightened. "Father's," she said. "Aunt Flora is mother's. These are quite different. Maiden."

There could hardly be, Jerry admitted, a greater difference between any maiden aunt and Pam's Aunt Flora.

"You mean," he said, tempted irresistibly down a side path, "that Flora's got another one? Her eighth?"

"Sixth," Pam said. "Of course, months ago. I told you then. This one's quite old, apparently. Fifty, anyway."

Aunt Flora, Jerry pointed out, must be close to seventy.

"Sixty-five," Pam said. "But I think it's encouraging she's closing the gap. How do we happen to be talking about her?"

"The other ones," Jerry said. "The maidens."

Pamela North said, "Of course," but for a moment still seemed puzzled. Then she said that, anyway, they were coming. "This afternoon," she said. "They'll expect me to meet them and have hotels and everything. Aunt Lucy forgot to mail it. She says, 'Thelma wrote this Monday but I forgot. I hope it doesn't matter. Don't tell.' "

Jerry enquired what Pam meant to say. Did she, for example, mean to say that she had, this Saturday morning, got a letter from three aunts who were arriving this Saturday afternoon and expected hotels? Pam did. Had Aunt Lucy ever heard of the telegraph? Or the telephone?

"Well," Pam said, "she's the literary one, you know."

Jerry ran his fingers again through his hair and spoke

feelingly of non sequiturs. Most of the literary ones he knew, as a publisher, were entirely familiar with the telegraph and the telephone. They commonly sent the one collect and reversed charges on the other. They usually wanted to talk about the advertising, if it could be called that.

"Reading literary," Pam said. "Not writing literary. Although I think she used to do little poems. She's really sweet, Jerry. Thelma's the horsy one. Shall I try the Welby?"

Jerry nodded. She should, by all means, try the Welby. He could think, offhand, of no hotel more maidenly. "Particularly," he said, "the cocktail lounge." He remembered it and shuddered involuntarily. Then he snapped his fingers. He said he had them.

"Lucinda and Thelma," he said, "and—what's the other one?"

"Pennina," Pam said. "Grandfather liked things to end in 'a'. Because his own name was Aaron, I guess."

"Listen—" Jerry began, but then he said, "All right. Try the Welby."

Pam tried the Welby. She appeared to make progress.

"The Misses Whitsett," she said, and spelled it out. "Three of them. With baths and connecting if possible." She waited. "Wonderful," she said. "Thelma will like being across the hall." She listened again. She gave her own name; she said she was sure they could make it before six. She hung up.

"They're due at three five," Pam said," and we can bring them down here for tea and then take them over to the Welby." She looked at her husband's face. "By then," she said, "they'll probably want naps or something." She looked at Jerry's face again. "Really, dear," she said. "And they're going on to Florida Monday."

"In October?" Jerry said.

"Aunt Thelma likes to be forehanded," Pam said. "Probably it's something about a horse, really. Will you, Jerry?"

There was, Jerry started to say firmly, a manuscript he ought to go over. It was, he said less firmly, at the office. Until that moment, he said with even less confidence, he had forgotten it.

"All right," Gerald North said.

"We'll have a long lunch at the Algonquin first," Pam said. "You're a dear, you know. Some husbands would pretend they had the most unlikely things to—"

"All right, Pam," Jerry said, and smiled as he looked at her. Pam got up to get more coffee. As she moved, she intercepted the weary shaft of sunlight and was silhouetted briefly. Jerry's smile was enhanced. After all, he thought to himself, aunts or no aunts. . . .

Jerry North had prepared himself at lunch. Standing now with Pam behind a guard rope in Grand Central, waiting for a train from Cleveland, it occurred to him he might a little have over-prepared himself. It was a very warm afternoon for October and the three—well, call it three; ignore his half of Pam's third—the three cocktails for lunch encouraged drowsiness. He shifted his weight to the other foot, swaying slightly from sleepiness. (Of course it was from sleepiness, Jerry told himself. What else?) A man in uniform opened doors in front of the guard rope and Pam and Jerry, along with fifty or sixty other people, could look down a long ramp into semi-darkness. At the bottom of the ramp, people began to appear. A tall man, carrying a briefcase, began to run up the ramp, ahead of all the others.

"Always one of them," Jerry said.

He didn't know, Pam told him. Perhaps he was making a connection.

"For Washington," Pam said. "A courier. Vital documents in the briefcase. Top secret."

The tall man reached the guard rope, reached across

it, seemed to engulf a small young woman. Pam North said, "Oh." She said, "Isn't it nice, Jerry? So much better than documents. There they are."

Jerry looked down the ramp. He looked down at Pamela.

"At the bottom with the red-cap," Pam said. "The tall one's Aunt Thelma, of course. Your tie's crooked, dear."

Jerry straightened his tie. He looked down the ramp. It swarmed with people; the aunts were submerged. They waited. People reached the top of the ramp, looking quickly at the faces of those behind the guard rope, fanned out to either side of it.

"Even when you know there isn't anybody, you always look, don't you?" Pam said. "Just on the chance. Even if you've only been to White Plains." She looked up at Jerry, as if to make sure he was there. He indicated that he was.

The people who were arriving came up the ramp solidly, filling it from rail to rail. Some of them waved to people waiting at the guard rope, gestured toward an end of it; knots of arrivers and receivers tied themselves in the passageways and were bumped by suitcases. Those who were not met swirled around them, became anonymous in the station.

"There they come," Pam said. She waved.

The aunts came up the ramp, the tall one who was Thelma in a tweed suit, leading on. The second one was in a print dress, largely figured, and a small blue hat. "Aunt Pennina," Pam said, and waved again. Aunt Pennina waved back. A little behind her, and of about the same height but not by many pounds the same plumpness, was the third aunt. She wore a black silk dress and a pink hat. At least, Jerry thought, it must be a hat. "Aunt Lucinda," Pam said. "Where did she *ever!*" She waved again. It was impossible, Jerry thought—it was absurd—that he could ever, even momentarily, have forgotten the aunts from Cleveland. Particularly, he thought, Aunt Thelma, whose felt hat was uncompromising; Aunt Thelma who led on to the guard rope.

"Around the end," Pam said, when they were close enough. She gestured.

"Nonsense," Aunt Thelma said. She advanced directly to Pam and Jerry. She lifted the rope and ducked under it. She held it for Aunts Pennina and Lucinda, who ducked obediently. She looked commandingly at the red-cap, who said, "No'm," and went around.

"My dears," Pam said. "So nice!"

"I suppose," Aunt Thelma said, "you got the letter only this morning, Pamela? Since Lucinda forgot to mail it?" She turned to look at Aunt Lucinda, who smiled hopefully and seemed somewhat to flutter, who said, "Oh-Pam-dear-I'm-so-sorry" in one breath. Then she came quickly to Pamela and kissed her; then she looked up at Jerry and reached out and patted his arm and said, "Dear Gerald."

Jerry North said, "Hello, Aunt Lucinda. Didn't matter at all."

"Of course not," Pam said.

"Anyway," Aunt Pennina said comfortably, "we're here. That's the main thing, isn't it?" She kissed Pamela. "So pretty, dear," she said. "And your nice husband, too." She smiled at him.

"Hello, Aunt Pennina," Jerry said.

"Good afternoon, Gerald," Aunt Thelma said, firmly, evidently feeling this had gone far enough. "Where's that man got to?"

"That man" had circled the guard rope and come up to them, wheeling luggage on a hand-truck. He looked at Aunt Thelma and then, rather quickly, at Jerry North.

"You want a taxi?" he said.

"I presume—" Aunt Thelma began.

"Yes, please," Jerry said.

"—my nephew has brought his car," Aunt Thelma continued.

"No," Jerry said. He felt he should explain. "Too

hard to park, Aunt Thelma," he explained. He hoped
that what he detected in his own voice was not a note
of apology. "Taxi, please," he said to the red-cap,
more decisively than he intended.

"Whenever you're ready," the red-cap said, with
dignity, with forbearance.

The red-cap trundled off.

"Come Lucinda," Aunt Thelma said. "Pennina."
She led them after the red-cap. Pennina came second,
Lucinda turned and smiled, flutteringly, at Pam and
Jerry. Then she followed too. Pam and Jerry North
walked after them, side by side. Aunt Thelma, when a
cab was found, luggage loaded beside the driver, gave
the red-cap thirty cents and led the way into the cab.
The red-cap looked at her and seemed about to speak.
Jerry gave him a dollar. "Thank *you*, sir," the red-cap
said. Jerry found himself hoping that Aunt Thelma had
not heard him. Jerry was conscious of an odd uneasiness, almost of guilt. He straightened his tie and got
into the cab, sitting beside Pam on a jump scat.

"Thirty cents was quite enough," Aunt Thelma said
firmly from behind him. "There is no reason to spoil
people."

"I—" Jerry began.

"Tell us about Cleveland," Pam North said quickly.

"What?" Aunt Thelma said. . . .

Three cats greeted them just inside the door of the
Norths' apartment. They sat in a semi-circle, the two
flankers sitting taller than Martini in the middle. Martini looked up at humans from round blue eyes. Her
daughters, Gin and Sherry, looked up from crossed
blue eyes. Sherry, who was a soft blue-gray on face
and legs and tail, where the others were a rich brown,
tilted her head to one side. She appeared to be, with
some apprehension, regarding Aunt Lucinda's hat.

"Oh," Aunt Pennina said, "the beautiful kitties. The
sweets!"

"Cats," Aunt Thelma said. "Hmm."

"I always think of T. S. Eliot," said Aunt Lucinda. " 'Growltiger's Last Stand' you know. As the Siamese something or other something or other. Such a wonderful poet."

"Yah," said Gin, the junior seal point, drawing it out. "Yah-ow." Then, resonantly, she began to purr.

"I suppose," Aunt Thelma said, "you haven't *any* kind of a dog?"

Martini turned deliberately and walked away. The other two looked at her in surprise and then, obediently, followed her.

"It's one of the words she knows," Pam said.

"Nonsense," said Aunt Thelma. "Cats! Where's the bathroom, Pamela?"

In order, the aunts "freshened up." In order they returned to the living room, to iced-tea and cookies. The aunts removed their hats; Aunt Thelma removed the jacket of her tweed suit. They talked to Pam about relatives, to whom, so far as Jerry—relaxed in a deep chair, not with iced-tea—could determine, nothing of great moment had happened. He considered the aunts and discovered that, now that they were, in a sense, landed, he rather enjoyed them.

They were, he thought, all in their sixties, and perhaps Aunt Thelma was the eldest, although perhaps she was merely aged by authority. Otherwise, they could not easily have differed more.

Aunt Thelma was not actually tall, except by comparison and, perhaps, by carriage. She was wiry under the tweed suit, her face had been left out in the weather and her hands were brown and vigorous. Her gray hair, worn short, was vigorous too; she regarded the world, commandingly, through light blue eyes. It occurred to Jerry that she probably wore tweeds, in part at least, because a rough gray tweed, while it collects dog hairs, does not show them. Gin came into the room, walked directly to Aunt Thelma, and began to smell her shoes. Gin's nostrils vibrated slightly and she laid her ears back. She looked up at Aunt Thelma, perhaps to see if she were what she smelled like, and said "Yow-ah!" in a rather puzzled tone. Dogs beyond a doubt, Jerry realized. Dogs and horses. It takes all kinds, he thought drowsily.

"All right," Aunt Thelma said to Gin, firmly but without unkindness. "That's enough of that." Gin sat down and began to look at her.

"—as for Flora," Aunt Thelma said, continuing.

It was the little thin one who was the literary one, Jerry remembered—Aunt Lucy. She had been pretty, in a way still was pretty. Her small face was bright with interest in things; she looked quickly from one to another of the people and the cats, as if she did not want to miss anything and, somehow, as if she were hurrying to catch up, and as if to hurry so was somehow bewildering. She saw Jerry when he looked at her, and a smile ran to her lips, as if late for an appointment.

"Old maids' gossip," she said. "What you must think!" She stopped, still smiling. "The world of books," she said, happily.

"Oh yes," Jerry said. "Yes." Then he felt as if too quickly he had accepted the triviality of gossip. "Not at all," he said, wondering what he meant.

She weighed about a hundred, Jerry thought of Aunt Lucinda; she had given thought to the black dress and something, probably from the subconscious, to the pink hat. (She had taken it off, now, but Jerry still could see it on her curled, gray-blond hair. He thought, drowsy again in the warmth of the living room, that he would always see it.)

Aunt Lucy nodded, her bright eyes, her eager face, waiting—waiting, Jerry thought, for talk of books. He could not think of anything to say about books, except that they weren't, currently, selling as well as one might wish. He doubted if that would serve, so he merely smiled. Aunt Lucy smiled back and nodded, as if he had in fact said something, and then, quickly, began to listen to Pam, who was talking about someone named Felix, of whom Jerry had never heard, but of whom Pam spoke with evident interest and apparent familiarity.

Martini returned to the room, looked around it with the air of a cat who finds a room infested with people, and jumped on Jerry's lap, making a sharp comment which Jerry hoped he misinterpreted. She put claws, but only the tips of claws, into his knee for traction, and gave everyone slow, complete scrutiny through unwinking blue eyes. Jerry put a hand on her back and she swished her tail.

Aunt Pennina was about as tall as Aunt Lucy and must weigh fifty, perhaps sixty, pounds more. She had round pink cheeks; the skin of her face was like very soft tissue paper, very gently crumpled. Her small, plump hands, were prettily white; her hair was white and soft around her face. That she was not a grandmother was almost inconceivable. She should be pampering grandchildren and dispensing from a cookie jar. And she looked as if she had been in the Norths' living room for weeks, almost as if she had been there always. She ate another cookie, and this interested Sherry, whose interest in food was unfailing. Sherry walked over, loose-jointed, at the downhill slant of a long-legged Siamese.

"Nice kitty," Aunt Pennina said comfortably. "Want a cookie?"

Sherry, thus addressed, said, at rather too great length, that she would try, once, anything she could chew. Aunt Pennina held down part of a cookie and Sherry smelled it carefully. She smelled Aunt Pennina's hand carefully. She licked the cookie. Then, briefly, as if for politeness' sake, she nibbled at it.

"Pennina!" Aunt Thelma said. "What *are* you doing?"

"Feeding the kitty," Aunt Pennina said. "Such a sweet kitty." She was entirely unperturbed; she was unsurprised that Aunt Thelma should have asked to have described an action so obvious.

"Crumbs," Aunt Thelma said. "On Pamela's rug."

Pam said it didn't matter. She said you had to expect things with cats.

"Pete used to tear them up in handfuls," Pam added. "Rugs, that is. Is there any talk of their getting divorced?"

There was, it appeared. Jerry half listened, half dozed. Sherry left the cookie, went to lick Martini. Martini, abstractedly, licked her in return. Then Martini jumped down, turned over on her back and pawed at Sherry. Sherry leaped over her and went off down a corridor, her hind legs appearing to run faster than her fore. Martini took after her blond daughter. Gin turned and, for no reason apparent to humans, began furiously to wash her tail.

"—not that we *know* of," Aunt Thelma said. "Of course, one can't help—"

"—such a beautiful, strange story," Aunt Lucinda said. "He kills this senator. So full of *meaning*—"

"—you *must* have made them yourself," Aunt Pennina said. "I know in Cleveland we can't buy—"

"Jerry," Pam said. "Jerry, dear." Jerry woke up to realize he had been asleep. "He works so hard," Pam said. "Don't you, darling? All last night."

Jerry looked at her in surprise.

"The manuscript, dear," Pam told him. "It must have been three when you—"

"Oh yes," Jerry said. "Of course. The manuscript."

It must, Aunt Lucinda told him, be wonderful to be a publisher.

"Well," Jerry said, "yes and—"

"So many books," Aunt Lucinda said, her face bright at the thought.

There was, Jerry agreed, always that.

"In any event," Aunt Thelma said, "we must go. Pennina. Lucinda."

The aunts would not have any more iced-tea. Only Aunt Pennina would have another cookie. In the cab going toward the Hotel Welby, Pam suggested dinner later. Aunt Pennina nodded contentedly; Aunt Lucinda smiled brightly; Aunt Thelma told them they would be too tired.

"Tomorrow, then," Pam North said.

"Tomorrow," Aunt Thelma agreed.

"Except," Aunt Lucinda said, "there's dear Grace, Thelma."

"Plenty of time for both," Aunt Thelma said.

"Grace Logan," Aunt Pennina said, in her relaxed, contented voice. "You remember, Pam. Such an old friend, from the old days, you know. We always call on our way through. So lonely, poor dear Grace."

"Nonsense," Aunt Thelma said. "Her son's there, isn't he? To say nothing of that Mrs. Hickey. And the servants."

"It's not the same, dear," Aunt Lucinda said. "And it isn't as if she had ever read much."

"I—" Aunt Thelma began, but the cab stopped at the Hotel Welby and the driver knocked his flag down. He told them that here they were, folks. Jerry got out and handed down aunts. The doorman collected luggage. In the lobby, Jerry waited while Pam took the aunts aloft, feeling that it would be unsuitable for him to go where he might see beds in which maiden aunts would sleep. He waited ten minutes and Pam rejoined him.

Pam patted her husband's arm and said he had been very nice to the aunts. Jerry said he was sorry he had gone to sleep.

"It didn't matter," she said. "It was hardly noticeable."

Jerry thought momentarily about this and decided not to disturb it. Instead, he asked who Felix might be.

"Felix?" Pam repeated. "Oh—*Felix.*"

"Yes," Jerry said.

"Some sort of a second cousin or something," Pam said. "Why?"

Jerry didn't know why. He said he had never heard her speak of him before and wondered.

"For heaven's sake," Pam said. "I haven't thought of him in years. I wouldn't know him if I saw him." She paused. "He's just a relative," she said. "Everybody has them. Let's go to the Plaza. To celebrate."

"What?" Jerry asked.

"Jerry!" Pam said. "There doesn't have to *be* anything." Then she paused. "I guess," she said, "just not being a maiden aunt. Because, it would be so dull, wouldn't it?"

They went to the Plaza's Oak Room bar. It made, as Pam observed, a nice start.

The next morning, the Norths slept late. It was after three when Pam telephoned the aunts at the Welby to make definite the arrangements for dinner. But the aunts were not in their rooms.

"Of course," Pam said, hanging up. "I'd forgotten. Calling on Mrs.—what was her name, Jerry? The old friend?"

Jerry didn't remember it either. He didn't try. Pam said it didn't matter; that, indeed, it couldn't matter less.

2

Sunday, 2:40 P.M. to 7:10 P.M.

Grace Logan said, "But of course. You must" in cordial tones, listened a moment, said, "The sooner the better, dear" and replaced the receiver. She sat for a moment in the ivory and white room and looked at the ivory telephone. She rubbed her forehead gently with slender fingers in a gesture so familiar that its purpose no longer existed, although once it might have been, only half hopefully, massage to erase the lines that form on foreheads as, through years, one raises eyebrows in astonishment at the world, knits brows in puzzlement at it, laughs at it and laughs with it. When one has, within months, to expect a sixty-third birthday, one has had time to make many faces at the world.

Grace Logan did not, by some years, look so old as, during recent weeks, she had begun to feel. She was a slender woman of medium height; her body had almost the graceful roundness of youth, and the black dress she wore was artfully contrived; skilled hands had arranged the white hair which was so cleanly white, which contrasted so effectively with the darkness of her tailored eyebrows; practiced hands—in this case her own—had applied lipstick to lips which were still soft, not yet tightened by age. Grace Logan might easily have been thought a dozen years younger than she was, as at fifty she might have been thought a youthful forty. Paul had often told her that.

He had said, when he was very ill, when they both knew he was dying, that he had had the best of her, and that was true—was true for both of them. She thought of Paul now, with Thelma Whitsett's authoritative voice still in her ears; she thought of Paul, dead five years now, and thought "Poor Thelma" and then that it had been nobody's fault—not Paul's, not hers, not Thelma's either. She thought "I'm lonely" and then that Paul should be here now she needed him. Then Grace Logan, with many things to consider, pulled herself together and considered the most immediate. She went down two flights of stairs and told Hilda that there would be three guests for early tea. "The Misses Whitsett," she told Hilda, who said that she hadn't realized it was time for them.

"October," Grace Logan told her cook, who agreed that, sure enough, it was October.

"Regular," Hilda said and then, after a moment, "Almost like birds, aren't they now?"

Grace Logan smiled and nodded, and thought of the Misses Whitsett migrating like birds, passing through New York in mid- or late October on their way south, passing through again in late March on their way to Cleveland. Lucy would enjoy the idea, Grace thought; Penny might. It would not appeal to Thelma. Going up a flight from the ground floor of her immaculate, narrow house to the front living room on the second floor, she wondered, as twice a year she wondered, what she and the Misses Whitsett would find to talk about. The old days, probably—the days they had grown up together, played together on the broad, unseparated lawns of two sprawling houses, gone to school together. So long ago, Grace Logan thought; so dreadfully long ago. Then, as she moved about the room, caressing it as women do the rooms they love, the lines of worry formed again between her eyebrows and again, not knowing she did it, she tried to smooth them away with the tips of her fingers. So much is wrong, she thought; so much worries me. And people are so—so thoughtless. They help so little, try so little to help. Like Rose that morning, after four years.

"To call *me* selfish!" Grace Logan thought, and sat down quickly in an ordered, empty room. "And to go when I need her most!" And to go, she did not let herself quite think, but could not avoid a little thinking, leaving these doubts in my mind—these doubts about the boy. Grace Logan, who had stood up so well because she had the strength to stand up, erased the doubts. Everything she did for young Paul was what was best for him, and done because she loved him and he was all she had left. It was Lynn who made her mother hard; hardness was contagious. Rose was, of herself, gentle, understanding. All of it proved, if any of it needed proving, that she was right in the stand she had taken. But it left her alone.

If it hadn't been for the other thing—the obscure, puzzling other thing—she would have been patient enough to make Rose understand. She was too worried to be patient, that was the trouble. She—

She heard footsteps on the stairs and went to the door to greet her guests. Mary, the maid, was hanging their coats in the hall closet below.

Thelma led the way up the stairs and Penny came next and then, with the familiar eagerness on her face, Lucy. Lucy had really outdone herself this time. What a hat!

"My dears!" Grace said, patting Thelma's arm, putting an arm around Penny, reaching down toward the ascending Lucy. "My dears! How *nice!*"

"You've done it over," Thelma said, looking around the room. "So beautiful!" Lucinda Whitsett said. "I've always loved this room," Penny said, and sat comfortably down in it. "So homelike, for New York."

"She always does things so beautifully," Lucinda

said. "Even when we were little girls at home. Remember—"

That started them. Even Thelma, although with brief excursions into the problems of judging cocker spaniels, softened in the warm bath of memory. Lucinda thought, as she so often thought—and said—under similar circumstances, that they had been like *Little Women*. (And Thelma said, as she commonly said, "Nonsense, Lucinda.") Thelma remembered a pony Grace had had, and how she envied her the pony; Pennina remembered picnics on the joined lawns and a boy named Harry, unremembered by the others. "He thought you were wonderful," Pennina told Grace. "I wanted him to think I was." She smiled comfortably at the memory.

"Not the last time," Thelma said, a little bleakly, and Grace, rather precipitately, rang for tea.

"I," said Thelma Whitsett, "would like to use your bathroom, if I may."

It was characteristic of Thelma, Grace Logan thought as she said "of course," said that Thelma knew the way—it was characteristic of Thelma that she did not want to "wash her hands." Her avoidance of circumlocution, particularly in matters of greater significance, was an oddly pleasant thing about Thelma, Grace thought, watching the eldest of the Whitsett sisters leave the room, erect and single-minded. It left you knowing where you were, at any rate.

"Dear Mrs. Hickey isn't home?" Lucy said, filling a hiatus.

"I'm so sorry," Grace said. "She'd have loved—" But then she stopped. There was no point in temporizing. "I'm afraid Rose has left me," she said. "She's going to live with her daughter. Lynn, you know." Her voice changed a little, hardened a little, when she spoke of Lynn Hickey. "I suppose Rose felt—" She paused again and shook her head. "I don't really know what she felt," Grace Logan said, temporizing after all. "Perhaps she felt cooped up here."

"A very pleasant coop," Pennina Whitsett said, and Mary came in with tea, began to arrange it on a table in front of Mrs. Logan. "Very," Pennina added, looking at layered sandwiches, a napkin covering what might be—what turned out to be—hot biscuits; looking at chocolate cake.

Mary had forgotten the vitamin capsules again, Grace noticed. Or, perhaps, thought the occasion of sufficient dignity to justify departure from routine.

"It looks lovely, Mary," Grace said and then, "I wonder if you'd mind getting my capsules? In the medicine cabinet in my bathroom, you know." Of course she knew; she was merely—thoughtless. Grace sighed, and then remembered. "When Miss Whitsett returns," she said, but that was needless, because Thelma Whitsett then returned. Mary, after an inspecting glance at the tray, went.

"Goodness," Thelma Whitsett said. "What a lot of tea!" She looked at Pennina. "Remember, Pennina," she warned. Grace Logan poured tea; Mary returned, with a brown bottle, put it near Grace, and passed embroidered napkins, Haviland plates, sandwiches, biscuits, cups of tea. Conversation ebbed.

Grace Logan herself did little more than nibble at a sandwich, although she drank tea. She was so seldom hungry and, watching Pennina Whitsett, who ate with great propriety but without dilly-dallying, wished she more often were. Perhaps the vitamin capsules took care of it. They were supposed to. She lighted a cigarette, to pass the stipulated fifteen minutes between food and what was, presumably, concentrated health.

"Mrs. Hickey has left dear Grace," Lucy Whitsett said and then, to the offer of a cigarette, "No, dear, I'm afraid I never do."

"Left?" Thema said. "Why?"

"She wanted to go live with her daughter," Grace Logan said. "I'm afraid I'd begun to bore her."

"It took her a long time to find out," Thelma said. "Ever since Paul died, wasn't it? Five years?"

Thelma remembered when Paul died. What had she felt? Grace wondered. She said it had not been quite that long; Rose Hickey had come to live with her, as companion, as friend, about a year later.

"Four years then," Thelma said. "You'd think she could have found out in five minutes."

"I'm sure," Pennina said, and swallowed. "I'm sure Grace couldn't bore anyone."

"Nonsense," Thelma said. "Anybody can bore someone." She paused. "Not that I suppose Grace did," she said. "There must have been something else. Quarrel?" The last was to Grace Logan, not about her.

Grace merely shook her head, at first. But then she hesitated.

"Perhaps we had a slight disagreement," she said. "About—well, about her daughter and young Paul."

"You mean *that's* still going on?" Thelma asked.

"Not really," Grace said. "At least—"

"You mean it is," Thelma told her. "Well—why not, Grace?"

"So many reasons," Grace said, and kept her voice light. "They really aren't suited. She's so—" She paused, willing to let it go at that. But Thelma said, "So what?"

"Competent," Grace said. "So—so self-assured. And, I'm afraid, a little hard. Young Paul is so sensitive, you know. So—so gentle."

Thelma said, "Um-m."

"He is, really," Grace said, and unscrewed the cap from the brown bottle, shook a capsule into her hand. "Vitamins," she said, and repeated the phrase which had occurred to her a few minutes before. "Concentrated health."

"You look well enough," Thelma told her. "Don't

believe in dosing, myself. But I told you that last spring. A change might be good for Paul. Some responsibility."

"Dear Thelma," Grace said. "We can't make people over."

"Nonsense," said Thelma Whitsett, who thought you could; who thought that, very often, you should.

"And Sally," Pennina Whitsett said, as if she had not been listening, but offering a path leading away from disagreement. There was, she thought, so little reason for disagreement.

"Dear Sally," Lucy said. "And her wonderful husband. The one who writes."

"You make it sound as if she had a selection," Thelma told her sister. "And he writes about biochemistry."

"He expresses himself," Lucinda said. "So wonderful."

"I'm afraid largely in formulas," Grace Logan said. "Sally's—Sally's fine."

There was something in her tone, and she heard it; she had not been casual as she planned. She put the capsule between her lips and washed it down with tea. "She's out of town now," she said. "Otherwise, I'd have tried to get her over. She's so fond of all of you."

Thelma said, "Um-m" to that.

"Do you mean," she said then, "that she and that Sandford are splitting up?"

"Heavens no," Grace said. "Whatever made you think—I—I—"

She put her hand to her head.

"I'm afraid I'm not—" she said, and the words were oddly blurred. "Dizzy—I'm—"

But then she opened her mouth, as if suddenly the air in the room had failed, as if she were trying to gasp it in.

"Grace!" Lucy said, and, oddly, she was the first to move. "Grace! What—?"

But then Grace Logan's slender body moved convulsively, one foot kicked up and the neat shoe struck the tea table. A cup near the edge slipped off to the carpet, did not break, poured itself empty.

Grace Logan fell back in her chair; for an instant her body arched, then seemed to collapse. For a second longer her eyes stared wildly, as if she desperately sought help. And then there was no expression in her eyes. She gasped for air for a moment more and blueness came into her skin, making her face hideous.

"Heart attack," Thelma said, and she was up, now. "Get—"

"It's no use, dear," Lucy said. She was kneeling beside Grace Logan's chair. "I'm afraid it's no use now. And—and I don't think it's a heart attack, Thelma. Because—because she smells of peaches."

Thelma was beside the chair by then. She bent over Grace Logan's body.

"Pits, Lucinda," she said. "Peach *pits*. But that's—that's impossible!"

"It ought to be, Thelma," Lucinda Whitsett said. "Oh, it ought to be!"

Pam North telephoned the Hotel Welby at a quarter after five, seeking news of aunts and getting none. She told Jerry it was strange. "Because," she said, "six thirty is dinner time."

"My God," Jerry said.

He was told that once wouldn't hurt him, and expressed doubt that this was true. He pointed out that six thirty was in the middle of cocktail time. Then he brightened, and pointed out that, if this was to happen, they had better begin early. He hurried.

But they were only in the middle of the first when the telephone rang and Pam, saying "Here they are now," answered it. For a moment the voice on the telephone was strange in her ears; it seemed to shake, the words were hurried.

"Pam dear," the voice said. "This is Aunt Lucy. I—

I guess we can't have dinner with you and Gerald. Oh, it's so dreadful. You see, Thelma—"

"Aunt Lucy!" Pam said. "Something's happened? To Aunt Thelma?"

"Not yet," Lucinda said. "At least, I don't think so. I'm downstairs telephoning. They said it would be all right, but there's—I think there's one of them out there."

"Aunt Lucy!" Pam said. "What—"

"But they're so suspicious," Aunt Lucinda said. "And anyway, I don't think any of us could eat. It's all—all so dreadful!" The light, suddenly old, voice broke.

"Dear," Pam said. "Tell me. What's happened to Aunt Thelma."

"They—they're going to——Oh, *Pam!*"

Pamela North waited.

"—arrest her," Aunt Lucinda said. "It—it just can't be happening. It *can't* be!"

"Arrest her?" Pam said, her own voice rising. With her head she gestured to Jerry to get on the extension telephone in his study. He nodded, and went. "What on earth for?"

"Pamela," Aunt Lucinda said, "I'm afraid—dreadfully afraid—murder."

"My God," Jerry said, on the extension telephone.

"She *loved* Grace," Lucinda said. "We all did. The other—why, it was twenty-five years ago."

"Aunt Lucy," Pam said. "Who has been—you say, *murdered?*"

"Cyanide," Lucinda said. "It smells of peaches. No, of peach pits. Apparently it was in a capsule. It was supposed to be vitamins and—oh, Pam—she said it was 'concentrated health.' And—and it killed her. And Thelma had been in the bathroom and then they found out about Paul and there's a man from the district attorney's office and—Pam, what shall we *do?*"

"We'll come," Pam said. "Where are you?"

She was, they all were, at Grace Logan's home. It was just west of Fifth Avenue in the Fifties.

"West?" Pam said, doubtfully. It seemed improbable. But Aunt Lucinda was certain of that. A private house.

"It's between enormous buildings," Lucinda said. "No yard at all. Oh Pam, can you come?" And Gerald too, of course?"

They could. Pausing only while Jerry gulped what remained in his glass, they did.

"I'm so glad it's west," Pam said, in the taxicab. "Otherwise it wouldn't be Bill. Because he's west, you know."

Jerry hoped Aunt Lucinda was right.

"She sounds a little—" he began, and Pam said she knew.

"But," Pam said, "I've always wondered whether she really is."

About the address, at any rate, Aunt Lucinda was right.

The house was indeed west of Fifth, where few private houses any longer were. It was a four-story house and a narrow one; wedged between much taller and much broader business buildings, Grace Logan's little house stood with its elbows tight to its sides, a subdued little house which, normally, one might pass a dozen times and never see. But now a good many people were seeing it; they stood on the sidewalk across the street and stared at it, and at the police cars in front of it. Uniformed policemen told them to get along, now, nothing to see here. But they waited all the same.

The Norths' cab stopped in front of the house, and was waved on. But by then Pam North had the door on her side open and was getting out. "No, lady," a patrolman said. He looked at Jerry, "No soap, buddy," he told Jerry.

"Lieutenant Weigand," Pam North said. "It's my aunt, you see."

"Who's—" the patrolman began, but by then Pam North had advanced, and Jerry paid the cab driver and went after her. At the top of the short flight of stairs running down from the sidewalk to the little entry, Pam stopped and said, "Oh." She stopped because a large man with a red face filled the front of the entry, and spoke over his shoulder to another man behind him.

"Like I've told you I don't know how many times," the big man said. "You try to make it hard for yourself, Lieutenant. What more do you want?"

"I've no doubt—" the other man, who was only a little above medium height, who had a thin face and wore a blue suit and a soft hat canted a little forward, began. But then, looking over the other's shoulder, he stopped. He said, "Um-m."

The big, florid man turned and looked at Pam. After a moment, he grew perceptibly more florid.

"No!" he said. *"No!"*

"Good afternoon, Inspector," Pam North said, in a polite small voice. "Hello, Bill."

"Weigand!" Deputy Chief Inspector Artemus O'Malley said, in a great voice.

"Sir?" Lieutenant William Weigand, Acting Captain, Homicide West, said in a much smaller one.

"The *Norths!*" O'Malley told him. "Don't you *see* them?"

"Yes, sir," Bill Weigand said. "Hello, Pam. Jerry. What in the name of—"

"If you—" Inspector O'Malley said, riding over everyone and now dangerously florid.

"No sir," Bill Weigand said. "Surprise to me, Inspector."

"My aunt," Pam said. "She's my aunt."

Both Inspector O'Malley and Lieutenant Weigand looked down at her. So did Jerry North. Jerry ran the fingers of his right hand through his hair.

"You mean to stand there and tell me—" O'Malley began, and stopped, too full of words for utterance.

"I'm so sorry, Inspector," Pam North said. "I'm afraid so. Aunts, really. I—you see it was really Aunt Lucinda who telephoned and we both thought it was probably east until . . ." She paused for a moment. "It's so hard to tell with Aunt Lucinda," she said, and smiled up at the inspector.

"*Stop!*" Inspector O'Malley told her. "I—" Again he did not finish. "*Weigand.*"

Bill said, "Yes, Inspector?"

"I won't have it," O'Malley said. "I've told you a hundred times. You know what happens when you let them in. You *know,* don't you?"

Bill Weigand nodded and looked attentive.

"Gets all screwy," O'Malley said. "Doesn't make any sense. Gets so you can't understand the damn thing. I've told you."

"Right," Bill said.

"You know what to do?" O'Malley demanded.

"Right," Bill said.

"Do it!" Inspector O'Malley commanded. He moved forward, blindly. Pam and Jerry drew aside. Inspector O'Malley steamed up the stairs to the sidewalk. He stopped. "The Norths!" he said. "Good God." He went, blindly, toward his car.

"He certainly doesn't like us in things," Pam North said. "But we can't just leave Aunt Thelma."

"Look," Bill said. "It's Thelma Whitsett who's your aunt? And the other two?"

"Of course, Bill," Pamela North said.

"Not Grace Logan?"

"Heavens no."

Bill Weigand took a rather obviously deep breath.

"Pam," he said. "You realize the inspector thought you meant Mrs. Logan was your aunt? That otherwise, Aunt Thelma or no Aunt Thelma, he'd have had you thrown out?"

"Bill," Pam said, "I was perfectly clear. I don't—I didn't even know Mrs. Logan. But I've got to help the aunts."

"I—" Bill began, and then, suddenly, he smiled.
"Poor Arty," he said. "One of these days—" He did
not say what one of these days was to bring forth. He
said, "As a matter of fact, we'd have wanted you in
the end, since the aunts are yours." He opened the
door of the house and let the Norths in ahead of him.
In the living room a flight above, in the room in which
Grace Logan had died with such sudden violence, but
where her body no longer was, he amplified. He spoke
quickly, succinctly.

Miss Thelma Whitsett was, in a room on the floor
above, being interrogated by an assistant district attorney. The other aunts were waiting their turn. But it
was Aunt Thelma in whom the assistant district attorney was most interested, and in whom Deputy Chief
Inspector Artemus O'Malley was most interested.

"But why?" Pam said. "Why, Bill?"

He told her. Grace Logan had died as suddenly as
anyone dies after ingesting five grains or so of potassium cyanide, which turns to hydrocyanic acid in the
stomach; which smells then of the insides of peach
pits; which causes death by a kind of asphyxia and
causes it within minutes. A capsule containing potassium cyanide had been placed among capsules in a
bottle containing vitamins, which had been kept in a
medicine cabinet in the bathroom off Mrs. Logan's
bedroom. And—Thelma Whitsett had been in the
bathroom only minutes before a maid brought the
bottle down to Mrs. Logan.

"Opportunity," Bill told them. "Obviously."

"Bill," Pam said. "The maid. Anybody. It might
have been there for days. You mean to say the
inspector—? Of all the flimsy—"

Bill Weigand smiled faintly. He would admit, to
them, here, that the inspector liked things simple. He
hesitated.

"In this case," he said, "very probably too simple.
But—it's not quite that flimsy, Pam. There could be a
motive, of sorts. Not particularly good, as it stands.

But—how much do you know about your aunts, Pam?"

She knew, she told him, what people generally know about aunts who live in another city, who are seen, briefly, once or twice a year. They were her father's sisters; they had lived for many years in Cleveland; they had never married.

"Aunt Pennina was always going to," Pam said. "I don't know why she never did. Lucy, I guess never. And Aunt Thelma—I don't suppose she—" But then Pam stopped. She said she was trying to remember something.

"Right," Bill said. "Your Aunt Lucinda remembered it and—mentioned it. She said, 'But that's ridiculous. So long ago.' Something like that. So we found out what was long ago and ridiculous. You remember?"

"Aunt Thelma was going to be married," Pam said. "I remember that. It must have been—oh, twenty-five years ago. She must have been—oh, in her middle forties. But, he married someone else."

"Right," Bill said. "His name was Paul Logan. He married someone else, Pam. A widow named Grace Rolfe. Five years or so younger than your aunt, and very pretty. She wasn't pretty when we saw her an hour ago."

"Bill!" Pam said. "That's—that's grabbing a straw. Twenty-five years, Bill!"

Bill Weigand nodded slowly. He said twenty-five years was a long time, too long a time; that no sane person carried hate for twenty-five years; that there was no present evidence there had ever been hate.

"No sane person," he repeated. "The inspector grants that."

"You mean," Pam said, "he thinks Aunt Thelma is—isn't sane? That she came here to have tea with Mrs. Logan and brought cyanide in capsules? On the chance that Mrs. Logan would be taking capsules and—"

"No," Bill said. "She knew about the capsules. Mrs. Logan was taking them last spring when your aunts called on her. After tea, as today. Miss Whitsett agrees to that. All the Misses Whitsett agree to that."

"Jerry," Pam said. "Don't *you* see it's ridiculous?" Now there was a kind of uneasiness in her voice. "Brooding for years, getting more and more bitter until finally—" Then Pam North stopped, hearing herself.

"It could be argued, Pam," Jerry said.

"I know," Pam North said. "I just did. But I don't believe it, no matter who says it. I—"

But she was interrupted by a voice from the door which said first, "Listen, Loot" and then, in a different tone, "My God." They looked toward the door, and Sergeant Aloysius Mullins looked at them.

"I guess," Mullins said. "I should of known, because it's begun to go screwy, Loot. Hello, Mrs. North. Hello, Mr. North."

They said "Hello" to Sergeant Mullins.

Mullins still looked at the Norths.

"Right," Bill Weigand said. "It seems that the Whitsett sisters are Pam's aunts. So—"

"Oh," Mullins said. "Well, I should of known. This son of hers isn't where he's supposed to be, Loot. Turns out he never was."

Mullins looked again at the Norths.

"A screwy thing," he said, vaguely accusing.

"Sergeant Mullins," Pamela North said. "We don't even know who you're talking about. The son of—" She stopped abruptly. "Whoms scare me," she said. "Whose son?" She looked puzzled. "About whom are you—" she began.

"Never mind, Pam," Jerry told her, soothingly.

"Mrs. Logan's," Bill Weigand told both of them. "Go ahead, Mullins."

Mullins went ahead. He had not far to go. According to Hilda, the cook, Mrs. Logan's son had been spending the past week, and was to spend the next, with friends in Maryland. But he was not, had not been. A telephone call disclosed that.

"He could," Mullins added, "be anywhere. Around here, likely as not. Figure we should—?"

"Not yet," Bill told him. "Time enough later."

"All the same," Mullins said, "it's another screwy one. You can see that, Loot."

"It—" Bill began, and then again there was a sound at the door. Aunt Thelma Whitsett came through it, followed by Aunt Pennina Whitsett and Aunt Lucinda Whitsett.

"This," Aunt Thelma said, without preamble, "is utter nonsense. These *men!*"

One of the men was behind her. He was a slight, sharp man, with a briefcase under his arm. He looked at the Norths and then at Lieutenant Weigand.

"The Misses Whitsett's niece," Weigand told him. "Mrs. North. Mr. North. This is Assistant District Attorney Thompkins. Homicide Bureau."

He looked at Thompkins and waited.

"For the moment, Miss Whitsett isn't needed," he said. "Not by us." He looked directly at Aunt Thelma Whitsett. "Although," he said, "I am not convinced that you have been as helpful as you might be. And I don't want you to leave town."

"Nonsense," the leading Miss Whitsett said, in her firmest tone. "Tomorrow we are going to Florida."

"We've got *reservations,*" Aunt Lucy said, her face not bright but sad, her voice protesting. "We're *booked.*"

Aunt Pennina said nothing. She sat down and looked at the other two, and at the men. She waited, relaxed.

"If you try to go you will be," Assistant District Attorney Thompkins said and then, approving his play on words, "Ha!"

"Lieutenant," Aunt Thelma said, "tell your man not to be absurd."

Bill shook his head.

"As a material witness," the assistant district attorney said. "All three of you, if necessary."

"Oh Thelma," Lucy said. "He *can!* I read somewhere about a poor old man who—"

"Never mind, Lucinda," Thelma said. "We shall see about this." She looked, with disapproval, at Thompkins, as if he were a dog without pedigree and of regrettable habits. "I shall consult an attorney."

"By all means," Thompkins said. "I should." It appeared that Aunt Thelma did not abash him. "And," he added, "I'll have the train checked, just in case. What train, Miss Whitsett? Or plane?"

"Oh," Lucinda said, "we never ride planes. We—"

"Don't be stubborn, Thelma," Aunt Pennina said, unexpectedly to everybody. "Tell the man."

"Really, Pennina!" Aunt Thelma said. "Stubborn!" But then she told the man.

"I think now," Aunt Pennina said, standing up, "that we might go back to the hotel." She smiled gently at everybody. "I'm afraid," she said, "it's quite past our dinner time. And such a trying day."

Pam and Jerry went with the aunts; Pam after a moment's hesitation. As they started for the living room door, Thompkins appeared to brush them from his mind.

"So Logan's skipped," he said. "Hm-m. How about Sandford?"

"Coming," Bill Weigand told him, as the Norths started down the stairs. Then he went to the head of the stairs and spoke down to the Norths. "You want to call Dorian and tell her I've had it again?" he asked.

"Of course," Pam said. "Bill—"

"Later, Pam," Bill Weigand said. "When it clears a bit."

The police cars, except that which had brought Thompkins and his aides of the District Attorney's Homicide Bureau; except for Weigand's car from the Police Department's Homicide Squad, had disappeared. The crowd had disappeared. A single uniformed patrolman stood in the entry. He watched the Norths and the Misses Whitsett without surprise, or comment.

The street was empty, with that peculiar emptiness of a New York side street on Sunday. Jerry looked up it, shrugged, and started them toward Fifth Avenue.

They had gone perhaps twenty feet when a tall man, carrying a light topcoat, met them and passed. He was walking quickly, as if late for an appointment. Pam North turned to look after him, and was in time to see him go into the Logan house.

"I wonder who that is?" she said. "One of the family?"

Jerry shrugged.

"Probably Sandford," Pam said. "They were expecting a Sandford. Whoever he is?"

Again Jerry shrugged.

They walked on, almost alone in the block. But then, as if he had suddenly come into existence there, there was a man on the other side of the street. He was walking slowly, sauntering, as if going nowhere. Then, when he was across from the Logan house, his slow movement slowed still further. It ceased. Then, in the shadowed street, the man on the other sidewalk ceased to exist as surprisingly as he had come into existence.

"Jerry!" Pam North said, her voice low, almost a whisper. "He's following him! Did you see?"

It looked, Jerry North agreed, uncommonly like it. The cops were thorough tonight. Then a cab came with its top lights on, and Jerry flagged it down.

3

Sunday, 7:08 P.M. to 8:50 P.M.

Weigand, as the downstairs door closed behind the Norths, went back into the living room and said, "Well?" to Assistant District Attorney Thompkins who, after a moment, shook his head. Bill said he didn't either.

"All the same, it's a coincidence," Thompkins said. "Maybe the old girl had hated for years and finally boiled over. It happens."

"Right," Bill said. "Damned near everything does, Tommy. At the moment, though, I shouldn't think there was anything to go on."

Thompkins said "Nope" to that. He said it would be a help if the old girl turned up to have a reticule full of cyanide around, Weigand agreed that it would, and someone made vocal sounds of being present at the door of the living room. Thompkins and Bill Weigand looked at a tall, blond man, heavyish, with blue eyes spaced wide in an open countenance and a look of worry on the countenance.

"Barton Sandford," the man said. "This is a hell of a thing. You wanted me?" He looked at them. "I suppose it was you?" he said. "You're the police?"

Weigand told him who they were.

"A damned awful thing," Sandford said. "The poor old girl."

38

Weigand and Thompkins paid this obvious truth the tribute of a moment's silence. Then Weigand motioned toward a chair, said that in things like this, they had to find out all they could; that, inevitably, for a beginning, they turned to relatives. Barton Sandford nodded.

"So—" Weigand began, but Thompkins interrupted. He interrupted to say he would be getting along; he added, "Nothing's ready for us." Bill Weigand said, "Right," to that and walked with Thompkins to the door and out into the hall.

"Between us," Thompkins said, "I've got a date. You know how it is. Another five minutes and they wouldn't have caught me. Or if your inspector hadn't been sure he had it sewed up."

"He's a good cop," Bill told the assistant district attorney. "I'll give you he likes to get things sewed up. Who doesn't?"

Thompkins started down the stairs. He stopped to say that Weigand would keep an eye on the old girls. "The Misses Whitsett," he amplified. Again, Bill Weigand said, "Right." He said, "Leave it to us, Tommy. Don't you always?" Thompkins only waved, and went. Bill Weigand returned to Barton Sandford, who had risen, had walked to the windows at the end of the living room and was looking down at the street. He turned as Weigand came in. He said it was hard to believe. "This room without Grace," he amplified.

"I know," Bill said. He paused a moment. "Tell me what you can about your aunt, Mr. Sandford," he said. "That is, your wife's aunt. That was it, wasn't it?"

It was, Sandford said. He said he was sorry Sally wasn't in town; he said he was trying to reach her.

"My wife loved Grace," he said. "They were almost like mother and daughter, in some ways. She used to live here, you know, before we were married."

"Trying to reach her?" Bill said.

"She's—she's on a trip," Sandford said. He spoke slowly. "A—a kind of vacation, I guess you'd call it."

Then he reddened a little. "I guess that's what you'd call it," he repeated. "But I'll get hold of her."

He was, evidently, embarrassed; he was, Bill thought, speaking in euphemisms. The chances were that "vacation" meant departure, more or less permanent; that Sandford didn't want to admit it, perhaps even to himself. Well, Bill thought, I'm no marriage counselor.

"We'll want to talk to her when you do," Bill said. "Unless, of course, we've got what we need before then. Meanwhile—"

Meanwhile, Barton Sandford told what he knew about Grace Logan. It was considerable. He had been "damned fond of Grace" and had seen more of her than one usually sees of an aunt by marriage. He had been at her house often, even since Sally left. She had now and then visited his apartment and they had talked about Sally's disappearance. "Particularly—" he said, and then decided not to finish that. Bill waited, then led.

Mrs. Logan had been, for five years, the widow of Paul Logan. They had one son, Paul, Jr., who now was about twenty-three or twenty-four.

"Grace was almost forty when they were married," Sandford said. "Thirty-nine, maybe. She'd been married before and her first husband died. Logan was— oh, maybe ten years older. All the same, they had Paul. She hadn't had any children before and, so far as I know, he hadn't either."

Sally was the daughter of Grace Logan's only brother; both he and Sally's mother had died when Sally was about ten. Grace Logan had raised her.

"I don't know if this is what you want?" Barton Sandford said, interrupting himself.

"Neither do I," Bill told him, and offered a cigarette. "It would be simple if I knew what I wanted, of course. Meanwhile I want everything." He lighted his own cigarette. "Most of it won't matter," he added.

"By the way," he said then, "wasn't Logan about to

marry somebody else? A Miss Whitsett? Change his mind suddenly when he met your wife's aunt? Very suddenly?"

"I don't know," Sandford said. "I remember vaguely there was something like that. Of course, I didn't know any of them until I met Sally."

"Right," Bill said. "Go ahead."

"Logan had quite a lot of money," Barton Sandford said. "Left it to his wife, of course. I suppose you want that?"

"Yes," Bill said. "Go ahead."

"Who gets the money?" Sandford said. "I don't know, precisely. I imagine young Paul gets most of it. Maybe Sally gets some. Sally wouldn't kill her for it; I don't think Paul would." He looked earnestly at Weigand. "I can't think of a single damn reason anybody would kill Grace," he said. "Not a single damned one."

Nobody ever could, Bill thought. The victim never had any enemies; nobody would kill for money; it was always the same. And there was always somebody dead, for all that.

"Mrs. Logan had a companion," Bill said. "A Mrs. Hickey?"

"Rose Hickey," Sandford told him. "Where is she, by the way? It'll be tough on her."

She was dependent on Mrs. Logan? Pretty much so, Sandford thought. She was some years younger than Grace Logan; perhaps as many as ten. She was a widow, with one daughter, Lynn Hickey. "Who works in a store or something," Sandford said. "Fourth assistant buyer. Something like that."

So far as Sandford knew, Mrs. Hickey had no resources of her own. She and Grace Logan had been friends for many years; after Paul Logan died, Grace had invited her friend to live with her. Lynn was at school, then; apparently there had been enough money for that. When she finished school, she had lived with her mother and Mrs. Logan for a few months; then got an apartment of her own. Sandford didn't know where. He didn't, he pointed out, know most of this directly. It was hearsay through his wife. He had known Mrs. Hickey only moderately, from visiting Grace Logan; Lynn he had met once or twice.

"Then you wouldn't know anything about a quarrel—maybe merely a disagreement—between your aunt and Mrs. Hickey?" Weigand asked.

Sandford looked astonished.

"My God," he said, "you don't mean—"

He didn't mean anything, yet, Bill told him. They hadn't seen Mrs. Hickey. They would.

"I don't believe it," Sandford said. "Not from what I saw of her. She'd be the last person." But then he paused. "Of course," he said, "I didn't know her well. And I don't know about things like this." He paused again, smiled faintly. "Perhaps I know more about cells than about people. I'm a laboratory man, you know. Biochemist."

Weigand said it was difficult enough for anyone to know who was the last person for murder, or who the first. Nobody really knew about "things like this." Any opinion might be useful.

"She seemed gentle, the little I saw of her," Barton Sandford said. "I don't mean weak. Probably she had a mind of her own; she'd have needed it to live with Grace. I'd have thought she'd be a hard person to quarrel with."

"And Mrs. Logan?"

Sandford hesitated. Then he spoke slowly. He said that Grace had been charming, delightful, willing to do anything for anybody. And yet—

"And yet," he said, "in a way she may have been selfish, without knowing it. I mean—sometimes the things she wanted to do for people were the things *she* wanted more than the things they did. You see what I mean?"

Bill did. He nodded.

"Take Paul," Sandford said, leaning a little forward

in his chair, speaking carefully. "She'd do anything for the kid. Except turn him loose—let him go his own way, make his own mistakes." He paused. "Except let him grow up," he said. Then, again, he pointed out that he was only guessing; made again the qualification that he knew more of biological processes in laboratories than of mental processes outside them.

Bill Weigand told him he was doing fine.

"Don't get the idea I think she was domineering," Sandford said, still earnest, his wide-spaced eyes intently on Weigand's face. "Nothing like that. She was a fine person. She just might—" He stopped.

"Have rubbed someone the wrong way?" Bill suggested, when Sandford did not continue.

"Not that much," Sandford said.

Bill didn't answer that. Somehow, it was evident, Grace Logan had rubbed someone the wrong way— possibly, of course, merely by continuing to be alive.

"Do you," he asked, "know whether Mrs. Logan had been in touch with your wife? Since your wife's been on vacation, I mean?"

"Sally's written her," Sandford said. "Grace showed me the letters. But just 'I'm here for a few days, everything's fine.' That sort of thing." He paused again. "Wrote her oftener than she did me," he added, with a note in his voice half rueful, half bitter. "But that's nothing to do with this."

"Mrs. Logan wrote your wife?" Bill asked. "The point is, if they were close, as you say, if there was something troubling Mrs. Logan, or frightening her, she might have confided in Mrs. Sandford."

Sandford shrugged and spread his hands. He said he supposed Grace had written his wife. He supposed she might have confided, if she had had something to confide.

"The fact is, I don't know," he said. "At the moment it's all—all a little beyond me."

"You know where your wife is?"

Sandford flushed then. He shook his head slowly.

"Not precisely," he said. "In the middle west, somewhere. St. Louis. Kansas City. One of those places. She's driving.'"

She was, Weigand thought, apparently driving away from Sandford. But that should have, as Sandford said, nothing to do with this.

"By the way," he said, "do you happen to know where we can reach Mrs. Logan's son? There seems to have been some mix-up about his plans. He's not—"

"Lieutenant," Mullins said from the doorway. "Mr. Logan just showed up. He—you'd better talk to him, Loot."

Mullins stepped aside and let Paul Logan pass him into the room.

Mrs. Logan's son was slight, at first glance—and perhaps now particularly—he seemed almost frail. Probably, Bill thought, taking a second glance, the appearance of fragility was deceptive, was heightened by the delicate modeling of his face. When he was even younger, Bill thought, they must have called him "pretty boy," and he must have hated it. Now, still appearing very young—younger than he could be if Sandford's chronology was right—he was rather extraordinarily handsome. Now he was very pale, his face contorted.

"They say," he said to Weigand, his voice uncertain. "They say—mother—"

"I'm afraid so," Bill said. "I'm sorry."

"It's—it's hard to believe," Paul Logan said. He put a hand up to his forehead, rubbed with slim fingers between his brows. (Lynn Hickey could have told Weigand that, unconsciously, Paul had copied this gesture; could have called it symbolic.) "She was—" He broke off. *"Why wasn't I here?"* he said. "Why?"

"She died very quickly," Bill said. "Nobody could have done anything. There wasn't time."

"She was always so well," Paul said, as if he were groping in his mind. "She—you're here because she was killed?"

"Yes," Bill Weigand said.

"How?"

Bill told him. He said it was very quick.

"It must have been—agony," the boy said.

"It was very quick," Bill told him. "Only seconds. Nobody could have done anything."

"I don't understand it," Paul Logan said. "Everybody loved mother. It must have been—it couldn't have been planned." Then he seemed to see Barton Sandford for the first time. He said, "Everybody loved her, Bart."

"That's right," Barton Sandford said, his voice gentle. "That's right, Paul."

Grace Logan's son was, Bill thought, in no condition to be questioned. They would have to wait until—

"I didn't find her, Bart," Paul said. "It was the last thing mother asked me to do, and I was no good at it. No damned good." His voice was bitter.

"Find her?" Sandford said. "Find who, Paul?"

"Who?" Logan repeated. "Why, Sally. Didn't you know?"

"Not me," Sandford said. He added that he didn't get it. He looked at Weigand and his eyebrows went up and he shook his head slightly.

"We've been trying to find you," Bill told Paul Logan. "You were somewhere looking for Mrs. Sandford? Why?"

"Mother's—mother was worried about her," Paul Logan said, and his face contorted again, briefly, as he made the change in tense.

The younger man turned to Barton Sandford.

"She thought you were—well, too casual about it, Bart," he said. "That Sally must be in some kind of trouble."

"For God's sake," Sandford said. He reddened slightly. "Sally's my wife. Couldn't Grace ever—" He stopped abruptly. He said, "Sorry, Paul." He hesitated a moment, and said, "Your mother was hearing from Sally every couple of weeks. Sally was all right."

He turned to Weigand, and said he supposed it was obvious enough.

"Sally's left me," he said. "Not permanently, I think—I hope. She said something about things not working out right, that she had to get away for a while and think about things. I tried to talk her out of it, and couldn't. She took her car and promised to write and—and said she hoped she'd come back. It's nothing to do with this. I've told people she's on a trip, which God knows is true enough. She can take care of herself." He turned back to Paul. He said Grace should have known that. Again he said he didn't get it.

All Paul Logan knew, he said, was that his mother had become worried. Perhaps it was something in one of the letters. He didn't know.

"She knew how you felt," Paul told Sandford. "She said, 'Maybe I'm a foolish old woman' but—but she wasn't old. Not really. She—" He seemed about to lose control, then to regain it. "She asked me to go to St. Louis, where Sally's last letter came from—to find Sally and talk to her, and see—well, just see if she was all right."

"She's all right," Sandford said, and now his voice was a little harsh. "She wants to be left alone." He looked down at Paul. "Look," he said. "People grow up. Some people."

It was getting a long way from Grace Logan's murder, Bill Weigand thought. But he let it go; perhaps it was merely going the long way round, in some fashion not now clear. More probably, it was merely one of those things about people that come out when lives are slashed by murder; one of those things with no value, no application, of no use to him as a policeman. But he let it go. He listened.

Logan had flown out to St. Louis and been unable to find Sally Sandford there. She had written on the stationery of a hotel, but she wasn't at the hotel.

"And," Logan said, "she hadn't been. That's what they told me, anyway. No record of a Mrs. Sandford."

It had been, apparently, like stepping up for a step that wasn't there, coming jarringly, flat-footed, on an unexpected level. The boy—one kept thinking of him as a boy—must, Bill Weigand thought, have had words ready to say to Sally Sandford; have had a smile ready and a handshake ready. But there was nobody to receive words or smile or pressure of hand.

He had, Paul Logan said, tried one or two other hotels, without result. He had felt that, in some fashion, he was failing to perform a very simple task, and had decided it was his inadequacy, and inexperience, which were to blame. So he had hired a private detective to help. The detective, beyond more or less establishing that Sally, at least under her own name, was not at any likely hotel in the city, had not helped.

"Not likely to," Bill told him. "Even if he was interested in more than his fee. It's a big town. All he could do was ask around. The police—"

Paul Logan shook his head. His mother wouldn't have wanted that.

"Nor I, for God's sake!" Barton Sandford said, somewhat explosively. "Didn't it ever occur to you two that Sally's my—" He stopped again, reddening.

"In any event," Bill Weigand pointed out, "the fact you couldn't find her proves nothing, Mr. Logan. She may never have planned to stay in St. Louis, may merely have used the hotel writing room. It's common enough."

It was time, Bill decided, to end this journey down a side path. He got back to it.

Paul Logan was sure, to the point of vehemence, that his mother had had no enemies; was unable to suggest anyone who would want her death, or gain by it. Most of her money came to him, he thought; some went to Sally. (That either of them might be suspected did not appear to occur to the slight, handsome youth. Which could be naïve innocence but did not have to be.) Probably some sort of provision had been made for Rose Hickey.

"Then, as he mentioned Mrs. Hickey's name, Paul hesitated and looked puzzled.

"Isn't she around?" he asked.

Bill told him she wasn't, told him what appeared to be the reason she wasn't.

"Quarreled?" Paul said. "Mother and Mrs.—" But then he stopped. It was, Bill Weigand thought, as if he had been incredulous and then had remembered something, or thought of something, which sharply abated incredulity.

"You know what about?" Weigand asked. "Or can guess?"

"How could I?" Paul Logan asked. He pointed out he had been away for four—no, five—days.

Whatever disagreement the two had might have started at any time, Weigand told him. During the past five days, to be sure; as easily, a month ago.

"I don't know anything about it," Logan said. "You'll have to ask Mrs. Hickey."

"Right," Bill said. He added they were going to, that they had sent for Mrs. Hickey.

"They're coming here?" Paul asked, quickly.

"They?" Bill repeated.

Paul Logan looked as if he had said more than he had planned.

"I suppose I was thinking of her daughter," he said, after a moment. "Lynn. She'd naturally come with her mother, I'd think." He looked at Bill Weigand intently. "You'll be wasting your time with Mrs. Hickey," he said. "She wouldn't have anything to do with—with anything like this." He paused. "It must have been an accident," he said.

"Can you," Bill asked him, "suggest any way a capsule full of potassium cyanide could get mixed with your mother's vitamin capsules? Or, for that matter, any innocent reason for filling a capsule with potassium cyanide?"

Logan slowly shook his head.

"Right," Bill said. "Neither can I."

"Unless—" Barton Sandford said, and Bill turned to him.

"Unless someone planned to kill an animal of some sort," he said. "A pet dog, for example. I mean, that might account for the loading of the capsule. Theoretically."

"Very," Weigand told him. "Did your mother have a dog, Mr. Logan? Any kind of an animal she might want to dispose of?"

Paul Logan shook his head.

"What happened," Bill told both of them, "is that someone with access to Mrs. Logan's medicine cabinet put into the bottle of vitamin capsules a capsule filled with a lethal dose of cyanide. The purpose was to kill her. The poison capsule could have been put in yesterday; it could have been put in a week ago—two weeks ago, for that matter. The bottle was two-thirds empty. Originally, it contained fifty capsules. Say she'd take, at the prescribed rate of two a day, oh—thirty, thirty-five. There's your two weeks, since the capsule could be placed anywhere the murderer chose in the bottle."

He looked at the other two men.

"Which is the reason," he pointed out, "that there's no point in asking either of you, or anyone else, for that matter, where he was when Mrs. Logan died—or where he was yesterday, or the day before."

That was the trouble with poison, Bill thought. He mentally damned poisoners. They were, when they used something like cyanide, more merciful than most who killed. But they were also much harder to catch.

"Whoever killed your mother, Mr. Logan," he said, "had to have two things—access to the medicine cabinet; motive for murder. Access for a minute would be enough—we may find that a hundred people had it. You obviously did, Mr. Logan. You, Mr. Sandford?"

"Sure," Sandford said. "And the servants, Mrs. Hickey, her daughter. Any guest Grace may have had in the past two weeks who wanted to wash his hands, or her hands. There's a bath downstairs, two—I think it is—on the floor above. Grace usually suggested anyone use hers. It's more convenient."

"Right," Bill said. "So—"

"Come to think of it," Sandford added, "my wife's one of the few people I can think of who couldn't have planted the stuff. Not within the past two weeks. She's been away a month—month and a half."

"However," Bill Weigand told him, "you don't know where. So—you don't know she couldn't have been in, say, St. Louis, flown back here for a day, flown back there, continued her trip."

"Look—" Sandford began, standing up, very tall, flushed.

"You brought it up," Bill told him. "I'm merely suggesting the problems, not that your wife was here, Mr. Sandford. I'm merely stressing that, in cases like this, we fall back on motive."

And do we fall, Bill thought. And does a jury want more!

"We—" Bill started again, and this time Mullins interrupted him from the door.

"Lieutenant," he said, "Mr. and Mrs. North are here." He paused. "They've come back," he said.

Pam North was at the door behind Mullins and Jerry was behind her.

"Oh Bill," Pam said, "something—oh."

Bill said "Hello Pam," and waited.

"We called Dorian," Pam North said. "Right after we dropped the aunts at the Welby. She's all right, Bill."

"Dorian?" Bill repeated. "Was there supposed to be—?"

"We thought you'd want to know," Pam said. "We were going to call, but if there's one here it isn't listed. But the Plaza's just around the corner, anyway."

Slowly, Bill Weigand ran the fingers of his right hand through his hair.

"But you're busy with Mr. Sandford and—" Pam said, and stopped and looked at Paul Logan.

"Mrs. Logan's son," Bill told her. "And her nephew. Barton—" But then he paused in turn. In some fashion, Pamela North appeared already to know Barton Sandford. He looked at Sandford, whose face was interested but puzzled. It did not appear that he knew Pamela North. "Mr. and Mrs. North," Bill said. He did not try to explain them further.

Paul Logan sat down suddenly and covered his face with his hands.

"We're both so sorry," Pam said. "Such a dreadful thing."

She looked at Bill Weigand, and moved her eyes slightly, conveying something. It was not clear what; it was clear only that there was, as she said from the doorway, "something." Something not about Dorian, therefore about Mrs. Logan's taking off; something—of course. Something which concerned either Sandford or young Paul Logan. Bill was rather pleased with himself.

He motioned the Norths out into the hallway and up the stairs to the floor above. On the landing there, there was a telephone on a table.

"I told you there would be," Pam said to Jerry. "I think it ought to be a rule that everybody is. Democracy."

"Listed in the directory," Jerry told Bill Weigand. "As it happens, we aren't ourselves," he told his wife.

"Only because of the butler," Pam said. "And all those other people. The one with a dog to be boarded." She amplified. "Somebody put want-ads in, with our telephone number," Pam told Bill. "An awful joke, or something. So we came unlisted. Bill, you weren't having him followed, were you? Because he was coming here anyway."

"Who?" Bill asked.

Pam told him.

"At first," she said, "we merely assumed it was one of yours. But after we dropped the aunts, we wondered. Aunt Lucy thinks you're wonderful, Bill, incidentally. Thelma doesn't."

"After you dropped the aunts," Bill said.

"If it wasn't the police, who was it?" Pam said. "Someone you ought to know about, anyway. So we telephoned you. I mean, we couldn't, so we came."

The police had not been following Barton Sandford. Bill hesitated, used the telephone briefly. The district attorney's people were not following Sandford.

"A shamus," Pam said. Then she looked puzzled. "Only he looked sober enough," she added. "And not bruised. Of course, we didn't see him very clearly."

Bill Weigand got the details. Not for the first time, as Pam gave them, Bill noticed how clear she could be when dealing with the objective, how sharply see and remember.

"I'm sure he had been following Mr. Sandford," Pam said, as she finished.

"Right," Bill said. He was sure too. He was sure, also, that the follower had known his business. If he knew his business, he probably would be waiting across the street for Sandford to reappear.

"Oh, Mullins," Bill Weigand called down the stairs. Mullins came, was instructed, went down the stairs, unhurrying; went out, unhurrying, onto the sidewalk in front. After standing there a moment, he crossed the street. Disarmingly casual, he looked into the shadows. After a little he recrossed the street, went up the stairs to the third floor landing, said, "No soap, Loot. He's gone."

"He was there?" Bill asked.

"Somebody," Mullins said. "Long enough to smoke a couple of cigarettes. Camels. Looks as if he took his time." He looked at Pam and Jerry North. "Of course," he said, "we couldn't prove it. It's screwy." He paused. "Like always," he added.

"Sergeant," Pam said, "how can we help it? We just *saw* it."

"O.K., Mrs. North," Mullins said. Inadvertently, he beamed at her. He slowly erased the beam. "All the same," he said, and looked at Weigand.

It didn't fit, Bill thought. Or, did it? Perhaps Sally Sandford had done more than leave for a trip. Perhaps she had left watchers behind. It would be doing it the hard way, with Reno the easy one. He asked the Norths to tell again about the follower.

The light had been from street lamps, leaving shadows. He had appeared and disappeared. A man of no characteristics outstanding in such light. About medium height; of medium weight; a soft hat worn to dip over the forehead.

"I had an impression he was well dressed," Jerry said. "I don't know why."

The man had, Bill thought, been adept at his trade, or lucky at it. He had waited for a time, then gone. If he were trying to find Barton Sandford in what might, sometime, be termed a compromising situation, he had known the Logan house was not the place for it, since otherwise he would have remained. The presence of the police car, which any private operative would have recognized, had not immediately thrown him off.

"The murderer?" Pam North said. "But what would be the point?"

Bill didn't know. He said so. Then he made up his mind and took the Norths back down to the living room below.

"Mr. Sandford," he said, "Mr. and Mrs. North passed you as you were coming here. They think you were being followed."

Barton Sandford looked at them blankly.

"Followed?" he repeated. "What the hell for?" He shook his head. "No reason to follow me," he told them.

"Your wife," Bill said, "might conceivably have hired private detectives. For obvious reasons."

"That's impossible," Sandford said, flatly. "Sally couldn't—do anything like that. I told you, it hadn't come to that, anyway. Not by miles."

Bill asked him if he had anything else to suggest.

"Sure," Sandford said. "Your friends here dreamed it. Somebody happened along after me, maybe. There are a lot of people in New York. Who'd follow me? What would be the point?"

"You can't think of any?"

"Look," Sandford said. "I'm a biochemist. Nobody important. Sure, my wife's aunt has been murdered. And my wife's off somewhere making up her mind about something. What's in any of that to make some guy follow me?" He looked again at the Norths. "They dreamed it up," he said.

"Right," Bill said. "They dreamed it up. But, I never knew them to before."

"We—" Pam began, with some firmness, but Bill moved fingers at her and she stopped.

"All right, Mr. Sandford," Bill said. "That's all for now. You're going back to your place?"

He was going to eat, Sandford said. Then, probably, he would go back to his apartment.

"Damn it," he said, "I'd like to help on this."

He hesitated, uncertainly, as if half expecting to be asked to stay and help. But he was told only that, when there was a way he could help, he would be asked to. He left, then. A detective from the precinct, briefed by Mullins, drifted after him, keeping an eye out for any other drifter.

It was, Bill Weigand said, as good a time as any to get something to eat. When Mrs. Hickey showed up, she was to be asked to wait. With the Norths, Bill Weigand went to a restaurant they had recently discovered on Central Park South, where martinis were crisply cold and filet mignon was thinly sliced and tender beyond anything which seemed likely; where service was rapid, if you wanted it so.

When they had finished, stood outside in the dim, warm night, Bill hesitated, and the Norths waited.

"You may as well come back with me," Bill said, then. "After all, Pam's aunt—"

It was as good a reason as came to mind, since policemen do not overtly solicit the aid of observant amateur eyes.

"And," Bill said, "the inspector won't be there."

"That's something," Jerry said, and the three went back.

4

Monday, 12:05 P.M. to 3:15 P.M.

Monday was warm again, and bright, but at a few
minutes after noon Pamela North had thought of nothing to do about it. Mondays were unimportant days,
and might as well be rainy. Jerry was always early at
his office on Mondays, starting a new week with a new
rush and a brisker than normal determination. It always interested Pam North to notice that by Fridays,
and sometimes even by Thursdays, the need for
prompt arrival, for going at things with a will, apparently had lessened. Possibly, she sometimes
thought, authors boiled up on Mondays; just as possibly, only publishers did—or perhaps only Gerald
North, who on Mondays was almost entirely North
Books, Inc.

Pam sat in her living room, listening to the faint
sound of Martha's progression through the rest of the
apartment, and tried to read the *Herald Tribune*. She
had read first the account of the murder of Mrs. Grace
Logan, which seemed accurate except that the name
Whitsett was spelled with two "t's" in the second
paragraph and, compensatorily, with four "t's" in the
fifth. From this, Pam had gone on to what seemed like
the murder of the world and then, in the hope of
consolation, to Walter Lippmann. This was one of the
days, she noticed, on which he wrote as if he ought to

be President. (He had his vice-presidential days and even, sometimes, his merely senatorial ones.)

"He ought to be President," Pam told Martini, who was stretched up Pamela, a furry paw soft against Pamela's neck. "Either he or, come down to it, Jerry. Would you like to be a presidential cat? Live in the White House?"

Martini shook the end of her dark brown tail from side to side, and Pam said she probably was right. "Of course," she added, "before they fixed it up, it ought to have been a good place for mice." To this, Martini made no comment, beyond faintly purring. She was an introverted purrer, merely vibrating within. Gin purred for the world to hear. Pam, with the arm allowed her by the one they called Cat Major, tried to turn the *Herald Tribune* inside out to reach the editorial page, upon which she often read the letters to the editor, although rarely the editorial articles. But this caused Martini to move uneasily, and to quit purring and to open reproachful blue eyes, so Pam abandoned it. One should, Pam felt, try to preserve a sense of proportion. She managed, without moving too much, to reach a cigarette and get it lighted. She blew the smoke carefully over the top of Martini's head. She thought of murder.

There seemed, in connection with this one, either too little to go on or too much. A missing niece, who probably had nothing to do with it; a grief-stricken young man loosed tragically, almost surgically, from a safe dependence; a biochemist with wide-spaced eyes and open face and a tendency to flush readily; a man who was, for reasons not apparent, following the biochemist from place to place; a slim, decisive, pretty girl named Lynn and her mother, no longer slim and perhaps never decisive, yet in appearance oddly like her daughter. And, of course, Pamela's three aunts.

She wondered briefly whether to try to reach the aunts on the telephone, and decided not yet to disturb Martini.

"After all," she told the cat, who now was asleep again, "after all, they've gone to Wanamaker's. It always takes ages."

Then she smiled, remembering Aunt Thelma's remark when, at a few minutes after nine, just after Jerry's resolute departure, they had talked together on the telephone. Pam had suggested lunch.

"We're going to Wanamaker's," Aunt Thelma had told her, firmly. "If we can't go to Florida until tomorrow, we can at least go to Wanamaker's." She had then suggested that Pam might like to go along.

Pam had felt duty closing in a little inexorably, and wriggled free.

"It's because it's twins, I guess," Pam said. "But I always get lost and never find anything."

To this Aunt Thelma had said merely "Oh?" at first and then, in a puzzled tone, "I'm sorry, Pamela. The connection—"

"Twin buildings," Pam said. "Siamese, really, because of the bridge. Anyway, I have to wait for the maid."

Pam then suggested dinner and duty, having got her unexpectedly by the throat, chuckled evilly. Aunt Thelma had said that that would be nice, unless they were too tired. She had asked Pam to call later. Now, Pam decided, was not enough later.

She wondered what Bill was doing, and what he had made of Lynn Hickey and her mother, except for the obvious—that Lynn and Paul Logan were in love, the girl, under the strain of what had happened, rather irritable in her love. Probably, Pam thought, Lynn was often irritated with the boy—with his gentleness, with what was perhaps uncertainty and perhaps an inner lack of decision, with what clearly was, at least in obvious matters, a lack of self-confidence. Well, Pam thought, the girl is young; she'll have to learn about men, if she's going to marry one of them.

"Dear Jerry," Pam said aloud to Martini. "All the

same, I'm glad he's not, or not very, anyway. No more than the right amount."

Martini, as far as Pam could determine, understood this aside perfectly. At least, she flicked the end of her tail in sleepy comradeship.

You had only to see Lynn and Paul Logan together to know how it was with them, Pam thought. They had been together in the room when Bill and the Norths returned and so conscious of each other that the most casual enterer of the room became conscious of their consciousness. But they had been apart, apparently because Mrs. Hickey was there—a plump woman, no taller than her five-foot daughter, gray-haired, obviously worried. And, in the end, adamant.

It was true, she had admitted, that she and Grace Logan had had a disagreement, as a result of which she had decided to leave the Logan house and move in with her daughter. But the disagreement had been, for all that, a trivial thing.

"It didn't basically change the way I felt about Grace," Rose Hickey said. "Or, I think, the way she felt about me. And it was entirely personal, Lieutenant."

And there she had stuck. It had had nothing to do with anything which concerned the police; nothing, remotely, to do with what had happened. Bill Weigand was patient with her; patient, afterward, with her daughter.

"I don't know what it was," Lynn Hickey had said, her voice crisp. "If I knew, I'd tell you. She won't tell me."

"Nothing," Rose Hickey said. "A trivial thing. It would all—all have been straightened out if—if—" She stopped and her eyes filled with tears.

Beyond that there had been nothing. Rose Hickey had not known of anyone who had had, with Grace Logan, a disagreement not trivial—a disagreement vital enough to lead to cyanide. She, like any number of others, could have placed the poison in the medicine bottle. She had not. Lynn had been at the Logan house, to see her mother—and Mrs. Logan too—several times during the two previous weeks. For all she could remember, she might have been in the bathroom. She recorded denial of murder in a clear, quick voice.

Mrs. Hickey, when Bill shifted from the impasse, had known that Grace Logan was worried about her niece, Sally. But the worry had never been lengthily discussed; Rose Hickey denied knowing why Grace, although the girl wrote her regularly, still was worried about her.

"Of course," she said, "she may merely have wanted to straighten things out. Not actually been worried. She—Grace hated misunderstandings, and she was fond of Barton too."

Rose Hickey had not known that Mrs. Logan had sent her son to St. Louis. She had accepted the story that he was with friends in Maryland.

"You?" Bill had asked Lynn.

"I knew where he was," Lynn had said, and then her mother had said, "Why Lynn!" in a tone which had seemed that of surprise.

And with that, unexpectedly, Bill had ended it for the evening—ended the part, at least, about which Pam knew. The Norths had gone out of the Logan house with Bill, leaving the Hickeys there with Paul, and the Norths had gone home. Bill, probably, had not. Pam wondered what he had done.

The telephone rang then and Pam jumped. So, indignantly, did Martini. The cat landed four feet away and her tail magically enlarged. Then she spoke nastily to Pam and went out of the room.

But Gin, who had been out of the room, now dashed into it, rushing to the telephone, talking with the quick emphasis of an aroused Siamese cat. Sherry loped after her sister, moving slightly sidewise; doing what Pam always thought of as overtaking herself. She sat down to observe Gin, who stood by the telephone and spoke to it angrily; turned to Pamela and spoke sharply.

"I don't think it's for you, Gin," Pam told the animated little cat, and Gin said "Yow-AH!" in a tone apparently of disagreement. "Unless you were expecting a call," Pam told the junior seal point, and herself picked up the receiver. Gin leaped to the table to help, rubbing against the receiver in Pam's hand, speaking into it. Over this, Pam North said "Hello?"

"Mrs. North?" a man's unknown voice said, and Pam admitted it. "This is Barton Sandford," the voice said. "Mrs. Logan's nephew."

Pam said, "Oh" and then, after a second, "Yes, Mr. Sandford?"

Sandford said that this was an imposition and Pam said, conventionally, "Not at all," not knowing whether it was or not.

"It's about that man you saw following me," Sandford said. "It's got me worried. I thought—I wondered if I could talk to you about it?"

"Well," Pam said, "I don't know anything, Mr. Sandford. Nothing more than that a man was."

"I know," Sandford said. "I realize that. But— sometimes things come back to people. You know what I mean? I thought if we talked about it there might—well, there might be something that would help you remember more than you realize you do." He paused. "Frankly," he said, "it's got me worried." He sounded worried.

Pam thought it would do no good. She said so.

"Maybe not," Sandford said. "Still, I'd appreciate it. Could you possibly have lunch with me somewhere?" He paused. "I realize it's a good deal to ask," he said.

"Oh, as for that," Pam said. "Not at all. Only—"

"You will?"

Pam hesitated a moment, thought "Why not?", her interest aroused. After all, she told herself, they are my aunts and realized she had spoken aloud only when Sandford said, "Sorry?"

"All right," Pam said.

"Fine," he said. "I know a little place in the East Fifties I think you'll like. Unless you've got—?"

"Of course," Pam said. "Wherever you like, Mr. Sandford."

He named the little place, and Pam had not heard the name; he gave the address and they agreed on one o'clock.

"Or a little after," Pam said.

"Yah-OW!" Gin said, this time directly into the receiver.

"One of the cats," Pam said. "Please, Gin!"

She was told it was good of her, and was appreciated; said "Oh, not at all," which seemed the only thing to say. As a matter of fact, she added, replacing the receiver, absently scratching Gin behind the ears, it is good of me. Damn good of me. Then she called the aunts again. Wanamaker's apparently had engulfed them. Pam showered and dressed and called Jerry, who apparently had been engulfed by an author and was probably in the Little Bar at the Ritz. "Engulfing," Pam thought, had her customary struggle at the apartment door with three cats, all of whom wanted to go too, reopened the door to tell Martha to be sure not to let them out when she went, herself lost Martini in the process, cornered her at the far end of the corridor, put her back in—almost losing Gin—and finally went down and found herself a cab.

"We certainly seem to have lots of cats," Pam said, absently, and the hacker said, "Huh, lady? Whatcha say?"

"Nothing," Pam said, and gave him the address.

"I said," Pam said, feeling she had been rude, "that we have lots of cats."

"Yeah?" the hacker said. "Well, s'long as you like 'em." It appeared he did not.

"Probably," Pam said, "you like dogs."

"Nope," the hacker said. "Can't stand dogs." He said nothing further until they had stopped at the restaurant in the East Fifties and Pam had paid and tipped him. "Don't like horses, either," he said then, and turned contentedly out in front of a truck, which swore at him. He swore back.

Barton Sandford was standing just inside the door, by the hat-checking counter on the left. He was even taller than Pam expected; he was hatless and in tweeds. It was not easy to think of him bent, in a laboratory, over—whatever was bent over in a laboratory. Pam was told that this *was* good of her, and said "Not at all." She was asked if she would like a drink, and said "By all means" in a tone unintentionally surprised.

"A martini, please," Pam North said. "Very dry, if they can, and with lemon peel. But just squeezed, not in."

There was a miniature cocktail lounge, a dining room beyond it and, from the dining room, stairs leading upward to a second floor. A maître d', who seemed to know Sandford, pulled chairs for them at a corner table in the cocktail lounge, delivered their drinks there. The drinks were not too dry and the lemon peel was in them. Pam was resigned and thirsty, thought that one can only dream of perfection, and drank. Sandford drank. He repeated that this was damn good of her. Pam repeated that she was afraid she could be of no help.

"Just a man," she said. "A—oh, a kind of medium man, very quick. On the other side of the street, where you wouldn't have noticed him, probably. I wouldn't have, except that when you went into the house, he first stopped and then—well, disappeared. Into an areaway, apparently."

Barton Sandford listened very carefully, as if he were hearing this for the first time; as if, from these bare details, he could make a picture, and an explanation. He nodded, as Pam finished, and said it was the damnedest thing. His pleasant face was troubled.

He shook his head, his eyes earnestly meeting Pam North's. He said that was the hell of it.

"I'm trying to find some sort of explanation," he said. "Any sort. Grasping at—anything. Bothering people. You, for example."

Pam avoided saying "Not at all."

"You see," he said, "after I left last night, I remembered about you and Mr. North. You—work with the police sometimes? I've read in the papers—"

Pam had given up trying to explain their status, which seemed to her at all times anomalous. "Working with the police" sounded as if they were informers of some sort. Yet, they did work—at least, they did much associate—with a policeman. It was—

"I suppose we do," Pam said. "In a way."

They sipped, while Sandford apparently considered.

"You see," he said then, "things like this don't surprise you, don't seem—well, so damned impossible. You probably have gotten so you expect strange things to happen."

"Got not gotten" Pam automatically corrected in her mind, and then said that she supposed in a way they had. For some years, anyway, things had happened.

That, Sandford told her, was precisely it. To him, nothing had, so that now it was all unreal.

"You jog along for years," he said, "and nothing happens. Nobody pays any attention to you; you do an ordinary sort of job. Any day might be any day. You see what I mean?"

Pam nodded, raised her glass, found it empty, put it down again. Sandford, without looking at him, motioned to the maître d' and then to the empty glasses.

"I work in this laboratory," Sandford said. "Nothing important. Research, but not important. Not big stuff. I go home at night and Sally's there. Maybe we go to a movie, maybe we go to the theater. We've got a little more money than most. That is, Sally has. But it's all—ordinary. You never stop to think about it much. You see?"

Pam nodded that she saw.

"Then it goes smash," he said. "Sally goes away somewhere and I'm damned if I know why. To 'think things out.' What the hell do you suppose she meant?"

He seemed to expect an answer. Pam could say only that women got that way, sometimes.

"Sally?" he said, as if Pam knew her and could tell. But now he did not wait for an answer. "Then Grace gets killed," he said. "Then you say somebody is following me. *Me,* for God's sake?"

The drinks came. Sandford drank most of his, seeming not to know what he did.

"It drives you nuts," he said. "I've got to find out what's going on."

There seemed to Pam North to be a kind of desperate anxiety in his voice; she felt he was trying to drag something out of her. But she felt there was nothing further in her to be dragged out.

"Apparently," she said, "this man waited in the areaway for—oh, ten minutes. Fifteen. Smoked a couple of cigarettes. Then went. Anyway, that's what Mullins thought."

He said it didn't make any sense.

"It wasn't the police," Pam said. "I'm sure of that. Actually, Mr. Sandford—" She paused and after a moment he said, "Yes?"

"I suppose the most likely thing," Pam said, and spoke slowly, "is that your wife actually wants a divorce and has somebody following you to—well, to try to get evidence."

Sandford finished his drink. Then he spoke decisively.

"I don't believe that," he said. "She couldn't do a thing like that. Anyway, she—" he paused. "She knows better," he finished.

He had, Pam thought, at least convinced himself, probably because he wanted it that way. She finished her drink, thinking that all the same, the man probably had been hired by Mrs. Barton Sandford. She declined another drink, and they went up the stairs to the second floor dining room. She felt that Sandford continued to expect something more from her, some assuagement of his uneasiness, some explanation of what had happened. She hadn't any.

"The FBI isn't after you?" she said, after they had ordered.

He laughed at that, said, "Not me" and then sobered quickly, urged another drink. Pam resisted temptation by a narrow margin.

They talked, then, inevitably, about the murder of Grace Logan. Sandford wanted to know if Pam's aunts were really worried, or had cause to worry.

"I was around to see Paul this morning," he said. "Rallying round. The kid's broken up, of course. The cook, Hilda, told both of us about the Misses Whitsett at breakfast. The cops must be nuts."

Pam didn't think the aunts were worried, or had cause to be, and Sandford reinforced this, heartily, with a "Hell no!" All the same, the cops were not necessarily nuts, Pam told him. The aunts had been there. Aunt Thelma could have put the poison in the capsule bottle. There was even a motive of sorts. Pam found herself sketching it. Sandford told her it was the silliest damn thing he'd ever heard, as the waiter brought vichyssoise. Pam agreed to this.

"What do the police think?" Sandford asked her, and Pam briefly raised her shoulders.

"Probably nothing yet," she said. "I'd think Mrs. Hickey might interest them. She won't tell what she and your aunt—aunt-in-law?—quarreled about."

"Oh," Sandford said. "That. Probably about Paul and Lynn Hickey. They want to get married. Lynn's mother was on their side. Lynn wants to make a man

of Paul, probably. He could stand having it done, don't
you think?"

"Heavens!" Pam said. "I only met him for a minute.
Isn't he made?"

"What?" Sandford said. "Oh—not entirely. Grace
coddled him. And, I guess, wanted to keep on doing it.
She thought Lynn was 'hard,' and wouldn't be good
for Paul. So—she thought, or pretended to think, Lynn
wanted to marry Paul because he'll inherit what Grace
had. She probably got around to telling Rose Hickey
that and—well, there'd be your quarrel."

"Is Lynn?" Pam asked.

Sandford looked puzzled for a moment. "Hard?" he
said, then. "No, I shouldn't think so. She can take
care of herself."

"And Paul Logan too?"

"Probably," Sandford said. "But I can't see either
Lynn or her mother doing—well, what was done. I
told the lieutenant that, incidentally. But of course, I
don't know. Maybe I don't know much about people."

They were at coffee, by then. He wanted to know
what the police would do next.

"Ask questions, probably," Pam told him. "Try to
trace the poison. Dig into things."

He nodded, abstractedly. He paid the check. He
said it was good of her to have come.

"I'm sorry I couldn't help," Pam North told him.
"But I told you I couldn't."

He said he knew. He said he had hoped there might
be something, anything; that he had hoped she would
remember.

"You see," he said, "I keep wondering if the two
things aren't hooked up, somehow—Grace's murder
and this man's trailing me, I mean. Because I'm certain Sally has nothing to do with it." He paused. "With
any of it," he said, his eyes insistent on Pam's. Pam
could not answer that, not being sure of anything
about it. She thought she ought to call the aunts.

"Just what you call a 'medium man,' " Sandford said. "Following me, waiting for me to come out, going away before I did. It doesn't make sense."

Abstractedly, she said again she was sorry she couldn't be more help. It had been just a medium man. She thanked Sandford for the lunch, wondering a little why he had asked her and why she had accepted. On the sidewalk she declined to be dropped anywhere, saying she was walking down to Saks to shop. She walked with Sandford west to Madison, where he was catching an uptown bus; she walked down Madison, looking in windows casually. She stopped at one to look at sports clothes, and was conscious that someone had stopped beside her. She walked on, found a store which promised telephones, and called the Welby from a booth. The aunts were still engulfed.

She left the booth and was vaguely conscious of a youngish man, well-dressed enough, looking at magazines in a rack by the door. Momentarily, she was puzzled that she had noticed him at all and, if at all, why with a faint consciousness of familiarity.

She walked on to Fiftieth and turned west in it to Saks and there walked through broad aisles to the stocking counter. She bought stockings and walked back across the store to men's handkerchiefs. She bought Jerry a dozen without monograms, was unable to find her charge-a-plate, although she was certain it was in her purse, and noticed a youngish man, well-dressed enough, looking at colored handkerchiefs at the other end of the counter.

"Well," Pamela North said to herself. "Of all things! Now it's *me!*"

It was unexpectedly unnerving. It was also somehow infuriating. Why, Pam North thought, the nerve of them—the very *nerve* of them! Then, impulsively, she started toward the front entrance of Saks, moving at a brisk canter. She'd show them, Pam decided, and emerged into Fifth Avenue, bumped into two people, said "Sorry!" and waved at a taxicab. Miraculously, it swerved in.

As easy as that, Pam thought, and gave the address of her apartment. There's—

The cab stopped at a light. Another cab drew alongside it. In the other cab a youngish man, well-dressed enough, was sitting comfortably, smoking a cigarette. He did not look in her direction. As a matter of fact, he looked away, so that she could not see his face.

"That man," Pam said, to her own driver. "That man's following me."

"Yeah?" the driver said, without turning. Then, dramatizing it, he did an over-elaborate double-take. He turned around. He looked at Pam North.

"Well," he said, after his examination. "Could be. I'll give him that, lady."

Unexpectedly, Pam North blushed.

"I don't mean that kind of following," she said. "I mean *following*."

The driver said, "Oh!"

"In the other cab," Pam said, gesturing toward it. But at that moment the lights changed and Pam's cab started forward with a lurch, so that the other cab was for the moment left behind.

"What I want to know," Pam's driver said, turning half around, apparently finding his way by supersensory perception, "is he going to shoot, lady? That's what I want to know. On account of, shooting I don't like."

"Of course not," Pam said, and then realized that she had no real ground for this optimism. For all she knew, shotting was precisely what the medium young man in the other cab—probably behind them now—had in mind. "Why should he?"

"Now lady," the hacker said, in a tone of weary reason, "you ought to know that. I'm just telling you, I don't like it. You got to figure he might miss. You give a guy a revolver, or maybe an automatic, and nine times out of ten he hits the wrong guy." He paused, went deftly around a bus, grazing it only slightly. "Like me, for instance," he said. "Especially if it's a big gun," he said. "A forty-five, maybe."

Pam was not frightened by this; she shivered, but she was not really frightened. Only, maybe a cab was a bad idea; maybe she should have—

"Of course," Pam said. "Take me back."

"Back, lady?" the driver said.

"Where you got me," Pam told him. "Saks."

The driver said, "O.K." and turned emphatically right in Fifty-fourth Street. He turned in front of a bus which was just starting up, and abruptly decided not to. The bus driver leaned out of his window and made remarks. He was still making them when another cab turned in front of him.

(It was the last of many straws for Timothy O'Mahoney, who had driven Fifth Avenue buses for years and never liked any part of it. "All right," Timothy said, "that does it." He opened the doors of his bus, picked up his change holder, and stepped out. Then he leaned back in. "We're not going no further," he told a busload. "You can sit or walk." As for Timothy himself, he walked. Timothy subsequently became something of a hero to the newspapers, if not to the Fifth Avenue Coach Company.)

By the time of Timothy's revolt, Pam's taxicab was half way to Madison, stopped in traffic. Pam looked back through the rear window. Another cab was immediately behind. It appeared to have a medium man in it.

"Here," Pam said, thrust a dollar at her driver, and departed his cab. She went across the street between two trucks, doubled back toward Fifth. While she was crossing the street, she heard a car door slam. She looked quickly; the medium man was out, on the left. He was waiting for a truck to pass.

Pam North, taking advantage of this momentary

curtain, doubled back again, this time toward Madison. She went east at a brisk trot, which interested other pedestrians. "You'll catch him, lady," a truck driver advised her cordially. "Just keep tryin'."

This isn't the way, Pam thought. This isn't at all the way. This way just *attracts* him. She slowed abruptly from a trot to a saunter, and was bumped into from behind. She turned to face her pursuer, and faced a very short, very fat man, very red in the face.

"Whyn't you watch where you're stopping?" the fat man enquired, puffily.

Pam said she was sorry, and started up again, finding an average between her two previous gaits. The thing, she decided, was to be nonchalant. She stopped to look into a window. She gazed with rapt interest at two bolts of tweed material, neither of which—she thought under her mind—would be good on Jerry. She looked, as casually as she could, back the way she had come. The medium man would be looking in a window. He was. He was looking with intensity at a display of one, no doubt perfect, hat. Pam, who had been faintly conscious of the hat as she flitted past it, thought of suggesting they change windows. She thought also of confronting her pursuer. Then she thought of her lack of any positive knowledge that he did not, indeed, have shooting in mind. Pam went quickly toward Madison.

She turned right there and did not look back. She walked to Fiftieth, west again, again into Saks Fifth Avenue. But this time she headed directly for the elevators as, she now realized, she should have done before. She wedged into one and, at the fifth floor—Women's and Misses' Dresses—wedged out again. She trotted briskly forward, then to her left, into the salon.

"Can I help madame?" a salesgirl in black enquired. She could; she had better.

"Something in wool, I think," Pam said. "And—

could you just put me in a dressing room and bring things in? I'm—" she paused. "Rather in a hurry," she added.

Into the dressing room no man, medium or otherwise—except, of course, a husband—could follow Pam. She took off her dress, lighted a cigarette, and sat down. She would show him; she had, indeed, already shown him. She sat in bra and nylon petticoat, relaxed. The salesgirl arrived with woolen dresses. Well, Pam thought, as long as I'm here. Anyway, it wouldn't be right not to. She began to try on dresses. There was a lovely one in a kind of rust color which, it was apparent to the salesgirl, particularly did things for Pamela North. As soon as she had seen Pamela North, the salesgirl had thought instantly of the lovely one in a kind of rust color.

It was wonderful. It was a hundred forty-five fifty. It was absurd. Pam tried on five other dresses, one of which was only eighty-nine ninety-five.

"But it doesn't really *do* anything for madame," the salesgirl told her. "A lovely dress, of course, but for madame—" She clucked slightly.

Pam tried on the rust-colored dress again. It really *did* do things for her.

"Well," Pam said, "I hadn't actually planned—"

"Madame will never regret it," madame was assured.

"Well," Pam said, "all right, I guess. Charge and—" Then she paused, remembering she had forgotten why she was there. "I wonder if you'd do me a favor?" Pam said. "See if there's a man outside?"

"A man?" the salesgirl repeated. "Oh—your husband, miss?" The salesgirl's voice lilted a little; it was, by and large, better to get them with husbands along. A man who could be brought along could be brought to almost anything—up to two or three hundred, often.

"What does he look like, miss?" the salesgirl asked, and Pam hesitated.

"Well," she said, "youngish."

"Of course," the salesgirl said.

"Sort of—well, sort of medium," Pam said. "Sort of not very tall, you know, but not *not* tall." She paused. Thinking of it, she had never seen—or partly seen—a man less easy to describe. "He looks like almost anybody," she told the salesgirl.

The salesgirl said, "Well," doubtfully, her hopes a little dashed. He didn't, she thought, sound like the two or three hundred dollar kind of husband. Some women are certainly casual about husbands, the salesgirl thought, and went. She returned.

"I guess he's the one," she said. "There are two of them, actually, but one's about sixty and with somebody. I guess the other's the one."

(Mr. Ralph Hopkins, the other one, an auditor living in Rutherford, New Jersey, sighed at this moment. He wished his wife would come out and show him another. Whatever it looked like, he'd say it was fine.)

"I guess," Pam North said, "I'd better look at something for afternoon."

5

Gerald North crossed the living room hurriedly when he heard Pam's key in the lock, and they turned the knob together from opposite sides of the door. Pam came in quickly, pushing the door to behind her, and said, "Jerry! The most awful—" precisely as Jerry said, "Pam! For heaven's sake—" Then they both stopped.

"Shopping!" Jerry said then, looking at his wife, who was wearing a rust-colored woolen dress and a hat he had never seen before. "While—"

"No," Pam said. "Oh, Jerry. Not really. It was just that I had to. Jerry, I've been being followed! It rubbed off on me!"

"Rubbed?" Jerry said. "Off?"

"The medium man," Pam said. "From Mr. Sandford. At lunch, apparently. As for shopping, what else could I do? Because he couldn't get into a trying-on room, naturally."

Jerry ran his right hand through his hair. He said, "Listen Pam."

"That way I shook him," Pam said. "Because, you see, he was expecting a blue dress and no hat, the way I had been, so this was really a disguise." She looked down at the dress. "Of course," she said, "it does do something for me, don't you think?"

"Listen Pam," Jerry North said. But he looked at her.

"It's a swell dress," he said. "Not that you needed anything done. Pam, is there a beginning?"

There was. Pam began at it; she took it step by step.

"Then of course," Pam said, "when the girl found he was still outside, waiting for me to come out of the trying-on room, I couldn't leave. So I had to look at more dresses. And then the hat department came around and I realized I didn't have anything to go with this one"—she indicated the dress—"so I looked at hats. The afternoon dress you'll love, Jerry. It's the very newest old-fashioned-looking and—"

"Listen Pam," Jerry said. "This was all while you were hiding from the man who was following you? I mean, the dresses and hat—" He paused. "Hats?" he asked, doubtfully. Pam shook her head.

"Only a new girdle," Pam said. "Except for the stockings, which I already had, and your handkerchiefs, of course. Oh yes—a slip. But the stockings and the handkerchiefs haven't anything to do with the rest of it. The disguise part."

"You went into the dress salon to get away from this man," Jerry said, a little as if he were counting. "You went into a dressing room because he couldn't follow you there. And, because you happened to be there, you bought two new dresses and a new hat and—"

"Jerry!" Pam said. "You *want* me to have clothes. And for all you know wearing the wool one out saved my life!"

"Listen, dear," Jerry said. "I think the clothes are fine. I want you to have clothes. It's just—" He ran his fingers through his hair again. "I guess it's just so damned impromptu," he said. "So—" Then he grinned at her. He told her the hat was swell too.

"All right," Pam said. "If you'd been me, what would you have done? Where would you have gone he couldn't come?"

Jerry told her.

"You can't stay in one of those for hours," Pam objected. "I mean, what would you do?" Jerry continued to grin at her. "And," Pam said, "what would I have done about a disguise?"

There was, Jerry agreed, always that. He thought, he told her, that she had acted very wisely. It had been, he told her, quick thinking. She looked at him.

"Really," Jerry told her. "And when you were disguised? So—becomingly?"

She had left the dressing room, gone down a long corridor, come out through another exit into the main salon. It had been empty by then, or empty of what mattered—the medium man. Pam had moved fast to the elevator, on the street floor fast again to the Forty-ninth Street door and a cab. So far as she knew, the medium man had not seen her or, in her new outfit, recognized her. She had come home.

"What we've got to do now," Pam said, "is get hold of Bill and—"

But now Jerry slowly shook his head. They'd get hold of Bill Weigand; in fact, he was then on his way to the apartment. They would tell him. But—

"You see, Pam," Jerry said. "Something else happened, while you were being followed. The aunts—it looks like the aunts are in trouble, Pam. For all I know, they're in jail. Aunt Thelma, anyway."

Pam said, "Jerry!"

"You see, Pam," Jerry said, "a couple of men from the D.A.'s Bureau dropped around on a hunch. Figuring they might find something. The aunts were out some place."

"Wanamaker's," Pam said. "How perfectly ridiculous. I mean, what did they think they'd find?"

"I don't know precisely," Jerry told her. "But, what they did find was cyanide. In capsules, in a bottle, marked poison. And—in Aunt Thelma's suitcase."

Pam's eyes were wide in her awakened face.

"Jerry," Pam said, "it can't be."

Apparently, Jerry told her, it was. The aunts had

returned to find the district attorney's detectives waiting. The aunts had been taken to the district attorney's office. Possibly they were still there, being questioned. Inspector O'Malley was there. Bill was, or had been. And, it was pretty much out of Bill's hands. For all Jerry knew, the aunts might by now be in the House of Detention for Women on Sixth Avenue. Unless by some miracle they had been able to explain—

The doorbell rang then in a characteristic rhythm. They let Bill Weigand in. He looked tired; he also looked worried. He admitted he needed a drink, and Jerry mixed martinis.

"He just told me," Pam said. "I just got home. The poor old things. But they've explained, haven't they?"

"How?" Bill asked her. "They've said they never saw the stuff before; that somebody must have put it there. In other words, it's a frame-up. Miss Thelma Whitsett appears to suspect the police; Miss Lucinda Whitsett is certain it was the murderer himself. Miss Pennina has no suggestions. Thompkins won't have any part of that argument, naturally. Neither will the inspector." He paused. "As a matter of fact," he said, "it's not so damn good, is it?"

"But of course that's what happened," Pam said.

She was told she was loyal.

"Why wouldn't it be possible?" she asked

Bill Weigand shrugged to that. Of course it was possible. Almost anything was almost always possible. Perhaps a jury would—

"No!" Pam said. "You can't let it go that far, Bill."

Bill Weigand accepted a glass; he drank.

"My dear," he said, "I'm a lieutenant, acting as captain. The inspector will settle for Thelma Whitsett; I imagine Thompkins will. For practical purposes, I'm out of it. Even if I believed your aunts, Pam—well, if the inspector and the D.A. decide they've got a case, what can I do?"

"You do believe them," Pam told him.

But then he shook his head. He said that, probably,

the inspector and Thompkins were right. To this, Pam shook her head firmly.

"Right," Bill said, and his voice was tired. "So— I'm not satisfied. Too pat in places, too obscure in others. The motive doesn't convince me. But the situation is the same. It's pretty much out of my hands." He finished his drink. "You see," he said, "O'Malley can call me off. And will."

"Listen," Pam said, "let them fit this in, Bill. I was followed all afternoon, starting with having lunch with Mr. Sandford."

She told her story. As she told about her lovely new disguise, Bill looked quickly at Jerry and they smiled companionably.

"Although," Jerry said, in reply to nothing spoken, "I don't know why *I'm* amused."

"You two!" Pam North said, and continued. "And," she concluded, "I didn't make it up. You know that, Bill. I don't do things like that."

"Right," Bill said. His tone was puzzled. "I suppose," he said, "they thought you were the other woman. Wanted to identify you. As a matter of fact, probably they did."

"How?" Pam said.

Bill told her. She had ordered, and charged, handkerchiefs at a counter. Without her charge-a-plate, she had given her name orally. The medium man was— how far away?

"But after that," Pam pointed out, "he still followed."

There was that, Bill admitted; there was that that didn't fit. He was told that none of it fitted; that, further, Pam did not believe it was merely a divorce investigation.

"All of it," Pam said, "has got something to do with it. Even the inspector would see that. As a matter of fact, I think I'll—"

"I wouldn't, Pam," Jerry said. "You know the inspector."

"What needs doing," Pam said, "is finding Mrs. Sandford. Instead of chivying poor old ladies merely because—" But there she stopped.

"Right," Bill said. "Because they carry cyanide around. And another poor lady died of it."

"All right," Pam said. "Why carry it around? Say Aunt Thelma used it and killed Mrs. Logan. So she keeps a whole bottle of it handy—for anybody who wants to look—in her suitcase. Labeled."

"I know," Bill said. "I said I wasn't satisfied. I'll admit I haven't been called off—yet. Also, I'd like to talk to Mrs. Sandford. She's in Kansas City, now. Or she was Friday."

Both the Norths waited.

"A letter came this morning," Bill told them. "Addressed to Mrs. Logan; signed merely with an 'S.' It said, 'Dear Aunt Grace: I'm driving on West. Don't worry about me. Tell Bart I'm all right and still thinking.' The envelope was postmarked in Kansas City, twelve noon Friday. We've asked the K.C. police to see if they can find her. Of course, she may have gone on by now."

"Actually," Pam said, "she may be any place by now." Pam pointed out the existence of airplanes. "Not that I would on a bet," she added. "They run into things. The ground, mostly." She paused. "Speaking of airplanes," she said, "why didn't the letter get here Saturday?"

That one had an easy answer. The letter had not been sent by air mail.

"Just signed with an 'S,' " Pam said. "But I suppose you checked the handwriting?"

The letter, Bill told her, had been typed. Only the signing initial was handwritten. But, before Pam got ideas, they had no doubt the letter was from Sally Sandford. Grace Logan had kept her niece's recent letters and several older ones, written before Mrs. Sandford had left her husband to think about whatever she was thinking about. The letters were all typed, and all, at the most casual glance, on the same typewriter—an old one certainly, a machine with the letter "r" canted to the right and the letter "e" perceptibly below alignment.

"We've checked with Sandford this afternoon," Bill said. "Showed him the letter. This was before we were told about the finding of the cyanide, incidentally. He identified the letter as from his wife; said the signature "S" was characteristic, and that he'd recognize the typescript anywhere. He said she always typed letters, on a portable Underwood she'd had for years."

"Of course," Pam said, "anybody who had the typewriter could write the letter. And anybody could forge a single initial, I'd think."

"Right," Bill agreed. "So?"

Pam didn't, she admitted, see where it got them. She merely said it was strange that there was a mystery about Sally Sandford, and at the same time a mystery about her aunt's poisoning, and Sandford's being followed.

"And my being," she said. "Also, about why Mrs. Logan and Mrs. Hickey quarreled. Mr. Sandford thinks he knows that, incidentally."

She told Bill about that. As she repeated what Barton Sandford had suggested, she suddenly stopped.

"Look," she said. "Suppose Mrs. Logan was right. Suppose the girl is, as Mrs. Logan thought, 'hard'—hard enough to—to eliminate obstacles. Particularly since, I suppose, Paul gets his mother's money?"

"Right," Bill said. "Sally Sandford gets fifty thousand. He gets the rest. Perhaps another two hundred thousand."

"Then," Pam said, "why not? The girl. Or the girl and Paul. Or the girl and her mother. Oh, when you come to that, just her mother?" She began to tick off on her fingers. "Or Sally, for the money or something we don't know about," she said. "Or even Sandford, so his wife would get the money? Or—"

"Because," Bill Weigand said, "your Aunt Thelma had cyanide in her possession, opportunity, a motive of sorts."

"Planted," Pam North said. "Anybody could have got into her room. I could have. There's a little suspicion on her, and the murderer wants there to be more, so he does."

Jerry pointed out that they were going in circles and went to make more drinks. The cats jumped to the chest to assist. Sherry put a paw on Jerry's hand, apparently to stop the movement of the mixing spoon; Gin happily smelled lemon peel; Martini made herself into a chunky boat, paws curled under her chest, and watched with enormous, unblinking blue eyes. Jerry spoke to her and she closed the eyes slowly and then reopened them. Gin, after apparently considering it, decided not to join the humans in a drink.

"All the same," Pam said, when Jerry had passed the drinks, "they *are* my aunts. If nobody else is going to help them, I am." She paused. "Oh dear," she said. "Probably they tried to telephone me when they came back and found the men there and I wasn't here, but out being followed. I'm sure Aunt Pennina would try to call me. Or Aunt Lucy. If they knew our number."

They did know that, Bill told her. Aunt Thelma had written it down, identified Pam's name, in firm, neat figures, on a pad by the telephone in her room. Whether they had, in fact, tried to call Pam, Bill Weigand didn't know. He doubted whether they would have been given the opportunity.

"Then—" Pam began, and the telephone rang. She answered it, handed it to Bill Weigand, who listened, said, "Right," said that they might be asked to keep at it for a bit. He put the receiver back.

"The Kansas City police don't find Mrs. Sandford at any of the likely places," he said. "They don't find evidence she's been at any of them, under her own name, anyway. They'll keep on checking. She ought to be told about her aunt's death."

Pam nodded. She said, "Bill, can I see *my* aunts?"

Bill was doubtful. He used the telephone again, Gin assisting. He asked, listened and looked a little surprised. "Well, that makes two of us, Tommy," he said. He listened. "Not the right two, as you say," he agreed. He replaced the receiver.

"Thompkins isn't satisfied entirely," he said. "He can't quite swallow the motive. The inspector's satisfied; the D.A. himself is satisfied. However, Thompkins has managed to get this much—the Misses Whitsett have been taken back to the hotel. More or less because they're too respectable for jail until everybody's damn sure. They checked Cleveland for the respectability."

"Of course they are!" Pam North said. "They're my *aunts!*"

The aunts would be watched in the hotel; had been advised to stay in it. Meanwhile, two detectives from the D.A.'s Bureau had flown to Cleveland to dig there into the past of Thelma Whitsett and Mrs. Paul Logan. So, Pam North could see her aunts.

"We'll all go," Pam said, and started up. Bill Weigand hesitated a moment. But then he said, "Right," and they finished drinks and went.

The aunts were having dinner in Aunt Thelma's room. Aunt Thelma offered coffee to Pam and Jerry; after a moment of, evidently, somewhat dour consideration, she included Bill Weigand.

"Although," she said, "it's nothing but hotel coffee." She paused. "*New York* hotel coffee," she added.

"Thelma thinks none of this would have happened except in New York," Aunt Pennina said calmly, buttering a roll. "I keep telling her—"

"Nonsense, Pennina!" Thelma Whitsett said, sharply. "There is no cause to defend New York. What I say is perfectly true. There would have been no such nonsense in Cleveland."

She looked sharply at Bill Weigand, ready to pounce

upon any disclaimer of this obvious fact. Bill merely
nodded with interest.

"In Cleveland," Aunt Thelma said, "the person is
considered. That inspector of yours, young man!"

It appeared that, in regard to the inspector, words
failed Thelma Whitsett.

"It's all just like a play," Aunt Lucy took the
opportunity to say. "The trial of somebody or other.
There was this young woman who was suspected of
murdering somebody and the young district
attorney—"

"*Lucinda!*" Thelma Whitsett said. "That inspector
of yours, young man. An entirely preposterous man!
Merely because I decided, after consideration, not to
marry Paul Logan."

"Aunt Thelma," Pam North said. "The cyanide."

"Someone put it there," Thelma Whitsett said.
"Obviously, the man who killed poor Grace for her
money. Anybody could see that."

"I read the most fascinating book once—" Lucinda
Whitsett offered. Thelma rejected her offer sharply.

"Well, young man?" she said to Bill Weigand. "Let
him speak for himself, Pamela." Now her voice, suddenly, seemed strained.

"Inspector O'Malley is an excellent policeman,"
Bill Weigand said. "He has every reason for suspect-
ing you, Miss Whitsett. He has, in fact, every reason
for charging you with homicide." His voice was mild.
"I have no idea what would be done about it in
Cleveland," he said.

"If this were not so inconvenient," Thelma Whitsett
said, "it would be laughable. Has this inspector of
yours any idea of the difficulty in obtaining suitable
reservations in Palm Beach?"

"Listen, Aunt Thelma," Pam said. "Listen all three
of you. You mustn't pretend this way. Don't you
see?"

And then Jerry North saw what Pam had no doubt
already seen; what probably Bill Weigand had seen.

Miss Thelma Whitsett was frightened. She was very frightened.

"Don't you see," Pam North said, "it won't just go away, my dears. It—" She looked at Bill. "Tell them," she said.

"Mrs. North is quite right, Miss Whitsett," Bill Weigand told Aunt Thelma. "It won't just go away. You can't push it away. It isn't laughable at all." He stood up and looked down at Thelma Whitsett. "Grace Logan is dead," he told her. "You were there. You saw her die. You could have killed her."

"No!" Thelma Whitsett said, and for a moment her resolute face seemed about to crumble. "Grace was— young man—Grace was—"

"Grace was a friend of ours," Pennina Whitsett said, when her sister's voice broke. "We wished only good things for Grace, Lieutenant Weigand. We were all girls together. We—we are old women now."

Her voice was very quiet. She looked at Weigand gently, very steadily.

"I'm sure you will understand," she said.

"—someone else," Lucinda Whitsett was saying then, and nobody had heard the start of her sentence. "It is like something I read once. There was this Mr. Gribland or some such name—"

Thelma Whitsett had recovered her composure. She said, *"Lucinda!"* in a sharp tone. Lucinda Whitsett said, "Yes, Thelma," and stopped.

"Miss Whitsett," Bill said. "A minute ago you said that it was you who decided not to marry Paul Logan. 'After due thought,' you said, or something like that. Wasn't it really that he—well, wasn't it he who changed his mind, after he met your friend Grace Rolfe? Whom he then married?"

"I—" Thelma began, but stopped when Pennina Whitsett spoke.

"Don't dear," she said. "Poor dear Paul—he wasn't what you thought, you know. It's been better as it was. But—but everybody in Cleveland knows, dear.

There's no use going on with it. Not with Pamela and Gerald and—and their friend."

"Right," Bill Weigand said. "Not with anybody, if it isn't true. Logan left you for Grace Rolfe, you hated her then and for years and—"

"And," Thelma Whitsett said, "went insane because I was jilted a quarter of a century ago? Bought cyanide somewhere? Killed one of my best friends?" Her voice was firm again, almost derisive. She turned to Pam.

"I'm sorry, Pamela," she said. "I'm afraid your friend's a fool."

"It's because," Lucinda Whitsett said, "all men think men are so important. It's in all the books you read. So if a woman doesn't—"

Aunt Thelma's *"Lucinda!"* must have come then by force of habit, Pam North thought. Because in a way Lucinda Whitsett was making perfectly good sense. She was even making very useful sense.

It was Bill Weigand, however, who answered. He smiled slightly at Lucinda Whitsett.

"You may have something there, Miss Lucinda," he said.

"Of course she has," Pennina Whitsett said, and found another roll and began to butter it.

But none of them was able to explain the cyanide. Miss Thelma Whitsett no longer, to be sure, insisted that the police had themselves planted the poison, being now inclined to join Lucinda in suspecting the real murderer. It was clear, however, that police chicanery remained, in Thelma Whitsett's mind, a distinct possibility. "Things happen in this town," she pointed out, adding that it wasn't like Cleveland. Pennina Whitsett said, reasonably, that she supposed it was the murderer, since who else would gain, and that it was too bad they had stayed so long at Wanamaker's, since otherwise they might have caught the man in the act. (All three of the Misses Whitsett seemed firmly to assume that a man had poisoned their friend.)

"If you hadn't insisted on stopping in the middle to have lunch," Thelma told her sister, "we might have."

"I got hungry," Pennina Whitsett said, equably.

But the three admitted that nothing was disturbed in any of their rooms; that, except for the poison tucked under clothing in Thelma Whitsett's suitcase, there was nothing to indicate an intruder. It did develop, however, that none of the Misses Whitsett had locked her door when she left the hotel, all of them assuming that the doors locked automatically behind them. "They do in Cleveland," Miss Thelma said. "It's the proper way." It was not, however, the way of the Hotel Welby.

"As a matter of fact," Bill Weigand said, "none of the doors was locked when the boys got here. There's that. It's a point for the—" He stopped abruptly, having too obviously been on the verge of continuing, "for the defense."

"It won't come to that," Pam North told her aunts. "I won't let it."

But when, having thus reassured the aunts, Mr. and Mrs. North and Weigand went down in the elevator, Pam found herself wondering just how she was going to avoid letting it come to precisely that. She was not encouraged when Bill, after checking in by telephone, reported that he had been told to take off the two days he had coming. If not official notice that the Logan case was considered closed with what they had, this was the next thing to it. "Ouch!" Jerry North said, and Bill said, "Right."

"I," Pam North said, with sudden decision, "am going to the Logan house. I want to talk to young Mr. Logan."

That was, Bill told her, between her and young Mr. Logan, who had, however, already been talked to. Pam said she had to start somewhere.

"And he's closest home," she said. "He's *at* home."

She was told by Bill Weigand, in a worried tone, to watch herself. Bill was told that that meant he didn't think it was finished.

"Since," Pam told him, "I don't have to watch myself from the aunts. Obviously."

"Right," Bill Weigand said, and then that he would, thus unexpectedly relieved, try to make a date with his wife for dinner. He started again toward the telephone booths, and Pam called after him. He returned.

"Why," Pam said, "don't you take Dorian to Gimo's? Then, if we can, Jerry and I'll join you."

Bill had never heard of Gimo's.

"A little place in the East Fifties," Pam said, and gave him the address. "Very nice."

Bill looked doubtful, feeling apparently that Pam North was up to something. He was told he would love it; he regarded her for several seconds and then said, "Right."

"The place I went with Mr. Sandford," Pam North told her husband in the taxicab. "The place I was followed from. I thought Bill might just as well case the joint."

She was told her idiom was showing lamentable indications of collapse, and that it came from associating with policemen. This Pam denied. She said it came from things she read.

"Like Aunt Lucy," she said. "Her mind must be full of jacks."

"Jacks?" Jerry said. "Oh, jack *straws.*"

It was, Pam told him, no time to quibble. They came to the Logan house. There was no longer a policeman there; there was no crowd there; it was again merely a house standing with its elbows cramped tight against its sides.

And Paul Logan was not, at that moment, in it. For a time there appeared, as Jerry pressed the doorbell, to be nobody in it. Then, as if from a distance, a square woman in her middle fifties, with blond hair pulled tight, with red cheeks packed tight and bright blue eyes, came to the door and opened it partially. Pam asked for Mr. Logan.

"He's not at home," the square woman said. "He went out to dinner."

Pam North said, "Oh."

The square woman began the closing of the door.

"Wait a minute," Pam said. "I remember. One of my aunts said something about you once. About hot rolls spread with something. Lobster newburg. You're—" Pam paused, having run out of a dim memory.

"Hilda," the square woman said. "Hilda Svenson."

"The Misses Whitsett," Pam said. "They're my aunts. They used to come here and have teas—wonderful teas. The most wonderful they ever had."

"That's nice," Hilda said. Then her round eyes grew rounder. "The Misses Whitsett," she repeated, the name sounding a little different on her tongue. "They were here—here—" Then the blue eyes filled with tears.

"It's so dreadful," Pam North said. "You were with her such a long time."

"Fifteen years," Hilda said. "Fifteen years last *March*. The Misses Whitsett are your aunts?"

"Yes," Pam said.

"Such nice ladies," Hilda said, blinking at the tears.

"The poor things," Pam said. "Now the police think they were the ones."

"Please?" Hilda said.

"That they gave the—the awful poison to Mrs. Logan," Pam North said. "At least, that one of them did."

"That iss not possible," Hilda said. She paused momentarily. "Nonsense, that iss," she added.

"And I thought perhaps Mr. Logan would remember something that would help them," Pam said. "I'm so sorry he isn't—"

"You come in," Hilda said, and opened the door wide. "This man. He is?"

"My husband," Pam said.

"A quiet one," Hilda said. "You both come in."

They both went in. They went to the upstairs living room and were asked to sit down, but Hilda stood. After persuasion, she sat too, to the relief of Mr. North. Pam North and Hilda agreed that the death of Mrs. Logan was a dreadful thing; Hilda's round blue eyes filled again with tears.

"They should be punished," Hilda said. "Whoever."

Mr. and Mrs. North agreed to this.

"We keep feeling," Pam said, "that there must have been something nobody knows about, or recognizes. Something before, you know, Hilda. Living here in the house, being so close to her, perhaps you can remember something?"

"What something?" Hilda asked, and Pam said that that was it, one couldn't tell. Perhaps Mrs. Logan had said something that now, remembered, would be important; perhaps she had seemed not herself.

"Worried," Hilda said. "She was worried. About that Sally. You know about that Sally?"

Pam did; Jerry did.

"She left that nice Mr. Sandford," Hilda said. "Some foolishness. When my husband was alive, there was no such foolishness. In the old country."

"Of course it is," Pam said.

"You young ones," Hilda said, and looked at Pam North with skepticism. She looked at Jerry North. "Don't let her," she told him. "Foolishness."

"I won't," Jerry promised.

"Listen, Mrs. Svenson," Pam said. "Was Mrs. Logan just worried about the whole thing? About Mrs. Sandford's foolishness? Or about something she was afraid had happened?"

"Please?" Hilda Svenson said.

"That something had happened to Mrs. Sandford," Jerry said. "Like being hurt, or ill?"

It was something about the typewriter," Hilda said. "There was something not right about the typewriter."

It took time to get more, and then it was not clear. At first, Grace Logan, Hilda thought, had merely been worried because of the foolishness of Sally's prolonged escapade. Later, the worry had apparently taken a different form. Hilda sometimes had to be guessed at; the Norths could guess that something had happened, three or four weeks earlier which, to Mrs. Logan, had given new, and more significant, meaning to her niece's continued absence. It was something about a typewriter.

"A machine one writes on," Hilda explained.

"Mrs. Sandford wrote her aunt on a typewriter," Pam said. "Was that the one she meant?"

Hilda did not know. Mrs. Logan had been elliptic; had said, as Hilda remembered it, that there was something wrong about the whole business. "The typewriter most of all." She had not amplified and Hilda had not asked more.

"I was cooking," she said. "She came to my kitchen and talked and sometimes I had to go on cooking. Things will not wait while people talk."

But, since Mrs. Logan's death, Hilda had been thinking and remembering, and that incident she remembered. After it, although letters continued to come from Sally Sandford, Mrs. Logan mentioned her more frequently, and seemed more worried about her. She had not, however, again mentioned the typewriter.

Hilda had not spoken of this memory of hers to anyone else, even to Paul Logan. For the rest she could add nothing to what she had already told the police, which told them little, except that Mrs. Logan's bathroom was much used by guests, was available to anyone in the house, so that almost anyone who got into the house could have substituted the concentrate of death for what Mrs. Logan had called "concentrated health."

It was almost eight o'clock when the Norths left the Logan house. Jerry, pointing out that they were drinks behind, suggested the Plaza, as no more than around the corner.

"Gimo's," Pam said. "We've got to tell Bill."

Jerry was doubtful.

"Don't you see?" Pam said. "It was the *wrong* typewriter. Whatever the police thought."

"Listen, Pam," Jerry said.

"What*ever* they thought," Pam assured him, and told Jerry the address of Gimo's, to relay to the taxi driver when they found him. They found him then. "The one Mrs. Sandford is writing on," Pam explained, when they had started. "Mrs. Logan noticed it."

It was a very short distance to Gimo's and when the cab stopped Jerry was still explaining that the police did not make mistakes about things like that, and Pam was unpersuaded, pointing out that anyone could make mistakes or take too much for granted.

The maître d' appeared to remember Pamela North, which was flattering. He offered an immediate table, but, told they wanted to look for somebody—"a Mr. Weigand," Pam told him—helped them look. They found Bill and Dorian Weigand, sitting opposite one another in a booth upstairs, eating veal scaloppine, and joined them.

"Bill," Pam said, "it's the wrong typewriter! Mrs. Logan found out and—and—" But there Pamela North stopped, and was puzzled. "Only," she said, "what does it mean? What difference would it make?"

When the Norths had been served drinks and had ordered dinner, when Pam North's suspicions had been explained, that question still remained. What difference did it make? There remained also Bill's complete assurance that the police had not been wrong. There was only one typewriter involved. All of the letters initialed by Sally Sandford and found in the Logan house had been written on that one typewriter. The defects were unmistakable, not to be overlooked.

"They stick out a mile," Bill told her. "The letter 'r' alone would be enough. Look, Pam, you could pretty near see it across the room."

"Tweezers!" Pam said. "That's what it is!"

The three of them looked at her. They looked at one another. They looked again at Pam North.

"All right," Jerry said, "I give up."

"It's obvious," Pam said. "It's the woods and the trees again. Not seeing whichever it is for the other. The one that's too obvious, of course."

They all waited.

"Bill," Pam said, "did real experts make the comparison? Of one of the typed letters with another? Or did somebody just notice the letter 'r' and the other thing—what was it? Oh, the letter 'e' out of alignment—and jump? Because either of those could have been done with tweezers and people see what they expect to. Or are expected to."

"Pam means—" Jerry began, but by then Bill and Dorian saw what she meant, and Bill nodded slowly. The imperfections which could be seen across the room, which were the obvious ones, could perhaps be faked. If not with tweezers which, Bill had years before discovered, Pam considered the universal tool, the inventive apex of the machine age, then with almost anything else. Possibly, in point of fact, with the fingers only. Identity in typescript would so be achieved, to the casual glance. With no reason for suspicion, none might enter the mind. If, nevertheless, suspicion had entered Mrs. Logan's mind—

"Right," Bill Weigand said. "I see what she means. As a matter of fact, I don't know. I'll find out."

He elected to find out then, although Dorian urged that he finish dinner. "He never finishes dinner," Dorian told the Norths, after Bill had gone to find a telephone. "He's supposed to be on his forty-eight. He—"

He had, Dorian told them, been telling her all about it. It had not been a restful dinner. Dorian wished Pam's aunts had stayed in Cleveland.

"Or," she said, "that Inspector O'Malley would go there and take the district attorney with him, and leave Bill alone to do his job. Or that he had a different kind of job."

"You've always wished that," Pam told her. "Only, not really."

"I—" Dorian began, and then stopped, her almost green eyes shadowed for a moment. Then she smiled and nodded and said Pam was right.

"You have to take them as they come," she told Pam, and the two women smiled together about the way they came.

"If you two would be happier alone," Gerald North said, formally.

"The way they come," Pam repeated, and both she and Dorian seemed momentarily amused. But then Bill Weigand came back from the telephone. There was an odd expression on his face and for a moment he said nothing. They waited. Bill did not at first seem to notice this; he seemed to have forgotten the errand on which he had gone.

"The typewriter?" Dorian Weigand said and seemed to be examining her husband's face.

"Oh," Bill said. "That." He seemed to shake himself out of abstraction. "I'm sorry, Pam. The idea's no good. They didn't stop with the obvious similarities. As a matter of routine, they made a thorough comparison. Everything they found at the Logan house from Mrs. Sandford was written on the same typewriter." He smiled faintly. "Nobody used tweezers," he said. "I don't know what bothered Mrs. Logan, but there was only one typewriter."

Pam North said, "Oh."

"What else, Bill?" Dorian said, still with her eyes on her husband's face.

"Else?" Bill repeated. "There isn't anything—" He looked at Dorian.

"Oh," he said. "I saw a man I know slightly. Didn't expect to see him here, is all."

But his tone was not convincing, and now all of them looked at him and waited.

"There's more—" Pam began, and Bill shook his head. Nevertheless, they continued to wait.

"All right," Bill said. "This much—and I don't know any more myself, and won't unless I'm told, and won't be told. The man I saw works for the government. He made a point of not seeing me, so he's probably working now. There's no reason to think it has anything to do with—with anything we're interested in. And—we make a point of keeping hands off, unless we're asked. They want it that way."

There was another pause.

"This is where Sandford brought Pam for lunch," Jerry said, his voice casual.

"Right," Bill said. "I gathered that. The martinis are only fair, so I imagined—" He broke off. He started again. "By the way," he said, "did you gather that Sandford came here often, Pam?"

Pamela North nodded, her face thoughtful. Then an idea crossed her mind and crossed, at the same instant, her expressive face.

"No," Bill Weigand said, "he's not here now." Pam's expression faded. "You can't have everything," Bill told her.

It looked, Pam North said, as if this evening she couldn't have anything. But then the waiter served her scaloppine.

6

Gerald North realized precisely what it was he wanted to suggest to the author of *Old Folks at Home*—in addition, of course, to the invention of a new title. The thing that had all along bothered him, Gerald North realized, was that, near the beginning of the ninth chapter, the time transitions, previously handled with so much dexterity, began to lose definition so that—so that—It was entirely clear in my mind when I started, Gerald North told himself. The time transitions from the ninth chapter on but Pam sees the woods even when most of us can't see the—no—no! The book I'm thinking about is Aunt Lucinda's Gribland's something or other and—he had it! The old folks aren't at home, Gerald North thought and realized that if he could only remember the phrase tomorrow the whole uneasy secret of the trouble with the tenth chapter would be—

"Jerry!" Pam North said, from the next bed. "Are you awake?"

"Of course," Jerry said. "I was just lying here—" He paused. "I am now," he told her.

Pam turned on her light.

"He's FBI," Pam said.

Jerry scrambled through his mind. What was it he had just hit on? He clutched at the fabric of a retreating

95

dream, and came back with meaningless words. "The old folks aren't at home," he said, half aloud, more than half doubtfully. What was that supposed to mean?

"Of course," Pam said, "if you'd *rather* talk in your sleep."

"I'm awake now," Jerry told her. "Who's FBI?" He remembered. "Oh," he said. "The man Bill saw at the restaurant. Of course, dear."

"Mr. Sandford too," Pam said. "Don't you see? It makes everything hang together. The man at the restaurant and Mr. Sandford are working on something." She paused. "Atom spies, I suppose," she said. "Even if they are dull. Anyway, that's why the other man was with him last night—no, it's Tuesday now, isn't it?—Sunday night. Not following him, but both working on the same thing. Mr. Sandford was going to join him, but they don't want the police in so he waited across the street, and then in the end had to go on about whatever it was they were doing. Mr. Sandford wasn't *being* followed. The reverse, if anything."

"Well—" Jerry said. "He seemed surprised. Sandford, I mean. At the suggestion somebody was following him."

"Of course," Pam said. "He would *seem* that, naturally. What do they call it? Cover. He wouldn't simply come out and admit it. But afterward he began to wonder whether I had recognized the man, or could describe him so that somebody else would—Bill say—which would have interfered with whatever they were doing. So he asked me to lunch to find out and—"

"Listen," Jerry said. He sat up in bed and turned on his own light. He looked across at Pam, a pleasant amount of whom was visible.

"Jerry," Pam said. "This is the important thing." She hesitated. "Right now, anyway," she said. "Keep your mind on it. Listen what?"

"Why would your being able to recognize Sandford's sidekick interfere with what he and Sandford are doing?" Jerry asked her, carefully. "After all, they're not after us."

"Nobody could know that without knowing what they *are* doing," Pam explained, making it easy. "I could think of a hundred reasons."

Probably, Jerry thought, she could at that. And— quite possibly one of them would be the right reason.

"All right," he said. "You can do that tomorrow. Why were you followed?"

"For the same reason," Pam said. "Just to make sure I wasn't on to anything—didn't go and tell somebody something. Like Bill, say, what Sandford really is, instead of a biochemist. When I tried to throw him off he wondered, of course, but I suppose when I just went to Saks he decided I was all right—" She paused.

"So you didn't really need the new disguises?" Jerry said.

"Well," Pam said, "I couldn't know I didn't. And tonight, this man Bill knows—probably the same one who followed me; the medium man—was waiting to report to Mr. Sandford. And—" But then Pamela North stopped suddenly.

"Jerry!" she said. "Suppose the man who followed me was on the other side? One of the atomic ones. He saw I was with Mr. Sandford, and wondered if I was an FBI woman and followed me to find out." She leaned toward Jerry. "Jerry!" she said. "Have I really got into something again?"

Jerry was now very much awake. But he did not know the answer to that question, except the prayerful answer that he hoped not.

"I've been lying here thinking," Pam told him. "Worrying. And you were sleeping so soundly, as if there weren't an atom in the world. Also, if we're going to be awake, oughtn't we to close the windows?"

Gerald North got up and closed the windows. He

got back into bed shivering. Somehow, he thought, things are always a lot worse when you are shivering. You feel defenseless.

"If it was the other ones," Pam said, "we don't know what to expect, do we? Anything—they might come here. They might—OH!"

There had been a fairly large noise from the living room. Mr. North tried to pretend there hadn't, but there had.

"Just something settling," he told Pam. "Things settle at night."

"Things?" Pam said.

"Buildings," Jerry told her. "Contraction and expansion or something."

"People break in at night," Pam said. "They—"

"All right," Jerry said, and got out of bed. It was still cold. Perhaps there was something to wearing pajamas after all, even if they bunched. Or leaving a dressing gown—

"Jerry," Pam said. "You're not going out there?!"

"Just something settling," Jerry said. "Sure. B-r-r!"

"Then I'll go too," Pam said. "Because if anything happened to you—"

"Stay right there," Jerry told her. "It's cold." But Pam was out of bed. In spite of himself, Jerry discovered there was consolation in this support. He told Pam to stay behind him, and opened the door of the bedroom. He opened it craftily. Three cats spoke as one—as one cat whose voice was changing.

"Sh-h-h!" Pam said. "Be—"

All three cats came happily into the bedroom.

"Oww-AH!" Gin said, exultantly.

"Who's there?" Jerry commanded the darkness beyond to inform him. The darkness was silent. Jerry touched a switch and the hall's darkness vanished; at the same time he stepped back inside the bedroom door, through which he had intrepidly ventured. He repeated his demand for identification, and got the same answer. Damn it, he thought, I wish I was wearing *something*. He advanced along the corridor, and at its end reached cautiously into the living room and flicked another switch tumbler. Nothing happened; whoever had left the living room last had turned off lamps at lamps, not, as was stipulated, at wall switch. Jerry advanced into dimness with what he hoped was confidence. He kicked a coffee table sharply, said "Ow!" indignantly, and found light.

The room was empty. There was nothing to explain the sound. "Set—" Jerry began, and then saw the martini mixer on the floor by the chest on which it should have stood. He pointed it out to Pam, who said, "Cats."

"Something settling indeed," she said. "I knew it wasn't that, anyway. I could tell it was something alive."

They returned to the bedroom, putting out lights behind them. When they entered, the cats went under beds. Gin and Sherry went under Jerry's bed; Martini went, aloof, under Pam's.

"Here Gin, here Sherry, here Teeney," Pam said. "Nice babies. Here Teency."

Martini made a low, interested sound; it was rather as if she were laughing softly.

"Oh dear," Pam said. "Now she's going to *play.*"

Jerry got down on the floor and crawled part way under his bed. He got Sherry by one foot and pulled and Sherry yelled. Gin watched with pleased interest and then went under the other bed to join Martini. By way of extenuating intrusion, Gin began to wash her mother's face.

Jerry put Sherry into the corridor, and closed the door on her, whereupon she howled. He went under Pam's bed and Pam, shivering, went into it. Pam said, "B-r-r, the sheets got cold do you want me to help you?"

Jerry reached in and both cats moved out of reach. He crawled further, and bumped bare shoulders on springs. He spoke soothingly to cats, who considered him with pleased expressions. He said, "Damn you both," and they appeared to smile. He said, "Nice Gin, nice Ginny, nice Ginger-cat," and Gin began to purr loudly.

"You look very funny sticking out that way," Pam told him. "You'll have—"

But then Gin, who could never resist blandishment for long, approached Jerry's wriggling fingers and—and he had her! He backed out, and deposited her in the corridor. He returned and crawled back under Pam's bed. Martini let him touch her smooth coat with the tips of his fingers. He inched toward her and she departed beyond reach, crouched, swished her tail. Her round eyes were large and, evidently, amused.

"Of course," Pam told Jerry from above, "she's just waiting for you to come around to that side, you know."

"So she can go out this one," Jerry said. "I know." He considered. "Lean out on that side and pounce," he said. "I'll block."

Pam leaned perilously out on the far side of the bed and pounced.

"Missed her," Jerry said. "More to your right."

Pam pounced again. Her fingers grazed Martini, who retreated from them delicately. Pam emerged further from her bed, hanging over it. She hung over so far that she could look under it and see Jerry. She greeted him cordially, and grabbed at Martini. She missed. But Martini retreated nearer Jerry. Pam grabbed again, momentarily lost her balance, and appeared to be about to stand on her head. She caught herself.

Martini moved. She moved toward Jerry, evaded his clutch, and went under the other bed.

"Of all the—" Jerry said, and came out himself. He started under his own bed, and Martini went out on the other side. She went to the door and sat down. She spoke sharply about people who kept cats, against their will, penned in bedrooms when all they wanted was to join other cats in living rooms. Jerry backed out, went around, and opened the door for her. She spoke briefly, rather impatient at the delay, and went out. Jerry closed the door.

"She has such fun with us," Pam said. "Where were we?"

"Somebody had just dropped an atom in the living room," Jerry told her. He shivered. He was told he would catch cold, and agreed. Getting back between the cold sheets of a bed long open would, he told Pam, be a grave risk.

"We mustn't take chances," Pam told him. "We don't want you catching cold. . . ."

An alarm clock wakened them, which it almost never did, and for a moment Mr. North was puzzled and resentful. Then he said, "Oh God, Philadelphia" and got up. Apparently he had somehow forgotten to reopen the window and thought he detected a slight headache. There was, he was relieved to notice, no signs of a cold.

"Not today!" Pam said.

Glumly, Jerry said, "Today. And I've got to stop by the office first." Authors and book and author luncheons, and the bringing of such together, did not wait on murder or even on the FBI. He told Pam to stay in bed; that he would pick up a bite somewhere. He spoke of "somewhere" in a tone indicating doubt of its existence, and was told not to be silly. He told Pam he oughtn't to let her, was relieved that she was unimpressed, and went to the guest bathroom, his in the absence of guests. While he was shaving, he heard the cats speak delightedly from the kitchen, which indicated Pam's presence there; the scent of coffee reached him as he tied his tie. "I stand upon a something something and tie my tie once more," he informed the mirror, thinking rather ineffectively of Conrad Aiken. "There are horses neighing on far off hills." There would also be authors neighing in Philadelphia, a less consoling thought. He went out to breakfast.

It was, Pam told him, funny how they had scared themselves last night, and the cocktail mixer, landing on carpet, was not even broken. He had, Pam told him, looked very amusing half under the bed fishing for Martini.

"About Sandford and the FBI," Jerry said, as he finished his coffee. "You might have something there."

Pam said it had been clearer the night before, but that she still thought she had something.

"Look," Jerry said, "I'll probably be late. I want to drop in at some of the book shops and introduce Ferguson. It's supposed to help." He paused. "Though God knows why meeting Ferguson—" he added, and paused again. "Will you—" he said, and then stopped entirely. Would she stay out of it; leave it alone? Would she let matters take their course, even if that meant the police took the aunts? Would she avoid involvement in what might, just possibly, be as dangerous as they had both, during the night, momentarily feared? He looked at his slim wife, who stood so well the grim impact of morning.

"Of course I'll take care of myself," Pam told him. "Don't I always?"

There was no time to argue that, since it would have required much time. Jerry got his briefcase, said he hoped she would and went. Pam poured herself another cup of coffee, and thought about what to do next.

The more she thought about it, the more probable it seemed that Barton Sandford was really an agent of the Federal Bureau of Investigation, posing as a biochemist. Or perhaps really a biochemist at heart, on loan to the government. Martini jumped to the table and Pam poured a little cream into a saucer; Sherry came up to investigate and Martini growled at her. Sherry jumped down, landing within inches of Gin,

who promptly hissed. It's peaceful here, Pam thought.
If it weren't for the aunts I wouldn't—

"For one thing," Pam told Martini, who industriously absorbed cream, "he looks like an FBI man.
Alert. Cleancut. Doesn't he?" Martini looked up
briefly and returned to the saucer. "Of course," Pam
said, "I never actually saw one. Except that one of
Jerry's, and then ony at the door." She paused. "Or
was he Naval Intelligence?" she asked Martini, who
did not look up.

Whichever he was, he had been the right type—the
Barton Sandford type. It had been during the war, and
he had come to interview Jerry about a friend of theirs
who wanted to get in something. He had, Jerry told
her afterward—the Barton Sandford type had been
leaving as she came home and had looked at her with
only mild suspicion—been a very careful man. He had
wanted to be sure he and Jerry were alone and, after
Jerry had told him they were, Martha had made some
kitchen noise. The Barton Sandford type had broken
off sharply, Jerry said, stared hard at the kitchen door
and then even harder at Jerry. *Alone, you said,* the
Barton Sandford type had told Jerry, and for a moment, Jerry told Pam, he had expected to be arrested.
The whole thing, Jerry was inclined to think, had done
his friend no good.

The point, if any, was that he had looked like Barton
Sandford, Pam told Martini. The same cleancuttedness, the same alertness. "The kind who look
ingenuous but apparently aren't," Pam told Martini,
who gave the saucer a final lick and jumped down. "So
probably he is."

But where that got her, Pam was not certain. She
collected the breakfast things and stacked them in the
kitchen for Martha; she went to shower and dress. It
seemed unlikely that Mrs. Logan had been killed as a
result of something in which the FBI would be interested. Apparently this was another matter entirely.
"I'm dragging a red herring up a blind alley," Pamela

North told herself, and dressed to go out. When she had dressed, she telephoned the aunts.

The aunts were, in a somewhat qualified fashion, still at liberty. Aunt Thelma had, however, caught cold.

"Always does when she gets upset," Aunt Pennina told Pam. "Lucy says its psychosomatic. Lucy's been reading about it. There's a policewoman in the corridor, I think. Will they arrest Thelma even if she's got a cold?"

Pam could only say she hoped not.

"That detective friend of yours," Aunt Pennina said. "He seemed sensible. Can't you give him a good talking to, Pamela?"

"Oh, I did," Pam said. "It's all right as far as he's concerned. But—"

"The district attorney," Aunt Pennina said. "That inspector."

"Aunt Penny," Pam said. "Mrs. Logan didn't have anything to do with atoms, did she? That you know of, I mean?"

"Good gracious, child," Aunt Pennina said. "Atoms? The ones that explode? What have they got to do with it?"

"Nothing, probably," Pamela said.

"As for poor Grace," Aunt Pennina said, "what would she have had to do with atoms? What—"

"I've got to go now, Aunt Penny," Pam said. "It's too long to go into on the telephone. Is Aunt Thelma taking aspirin?"

"Good gracious no, child," Aunt Pennina said. "I don't suppose she'll ever take any medicine again." She paused. "I'm not sure I will," she added. "With all this cyanide around." She paused again. "Poor Thelma is dreadfully frightened, Pamela," she said. "However she acts. I suppose you know that? And—we all are, Pamela."

"You mustn't be," Pam told her. "It—it'll be all right."

Aunt Pennina did not say anything. She made a small sound—like the catching of a breath, almost like a curbed sob.

"Aunt Penny," Pam said. "I won't *let* anything happen."

There was a pause, and the small sound again. Then, in a voice which was not quite certain, Aunt Pennina Whitsett said, "You're a dear child, Pamela. I hope—"

It was easy enough to say, Pam North thought, hanging up a few seconds later, hoping she had encouraged Aunt Penny, realizing how frightened the three elderly women were if even Aunt Penny's voice—and her fears—went out of control. It's easy enough to say I won't let anything happen. Of all the days for Jerry to have to go to Philadelphia!

She telephoned Bill Weigand, finding him at home. He knew nothing new, except that it had been decided not actually to arrest Thelma Whitsett that day, perhaps not until they had cleaned up the Cleveland end, which might take several days. But after that?

"I'm afraid so, Pam," he said. "Unless something new turns up."

"And," Pam said, "nobody's turning, are they?"

Bill hesitated a mome t. Then he said he was checking up on a point or two. More or less unofficially, he told her. Probably nothing that would come to anything.

"What?" Pam asked him.

"No," he said. "I'm sorry, Pam. It's—they're ticklish points, Pam."

"Bill!" Pam said. She was indignant. "When did Jerry and I ever—"

"Never," Bill said. "All the same—no. Not now, anyway." He paused. "I wish you and Jerry'd just—"

"Bill," Pam said. "The poor old things! You think I'd just let them—let the inspector and that district attorney—when you're just sitting there talking about mysterious ticklish points?"

Bill Weigand didn't. He said he didn't. He said, in a

different voice, that all the same he wished she would.

Pamela North, for the first time in her life, hung up on Bill Weigand, who said, "Damn!" unhappily, and then told Dorian that there were times when protective custody didn't seem like a completely bad idea.

"Incidentally," he said, "you used to want me to get off the cops. You could be going to get what you wanted."

"Wonderful," Dorian said. "If—if you want it."

"The last thing," Bill said. "Damn the Misses Whitsett." He leaned down and kissed Dorian, who put her arms around his neck and held him hard. "I'm going downtown and stick my neck out," he told her. "Maybe I'll come back without my head."

Dorian held the head in question against her body, and kissed the top of it and then let Bill go.

"Of course," Bill told her, "maybe they'll merely put me on a desk job out in Queens."

He was told he thought of the nicest things. He went.

For a minute or two after he had left, Dorian Weigand sat curled as she had been in a corner of the sofa. Then she uncurled and stood up, all in one unbroken movement, and walked across the room to the telephone. She moved with singular grace. She sat down at the telephone and dialed the number of the Norths' apartment. She had almost given up when Pam answered.

"Dorian," Pam said, "tell Bill I didn't mean to hang up on him. Or, I did then but I don't now. I was so long because I'd just gone out when the bell started and I couldn't find the key at first. You know."

Dorian said she knew.

"Pam," she said, "you are going to go on with it? In spite of what Bill said?"

"I have to," Pam told her. "The aunts. And Jerry's picked today to have to go to Philadelphia."

"Then," Dorian Weigand said, "maybe I can help? Anyway, keep you company. Shall I?"

"That," Pam North told her, "would be wonderful. *We'll* show them."

But when they were together, when Pam had said, "Um-m, new hat" and Dorian had said, more doubtfully, "Do you really like it? Bill says—," it was not immediately apparent what they were going to show to whom.

"Don't tell me secrets," Pam said, "unless you want to, of course, but is Bill really on to something?"

Something, yes; what, Dorian didn't know. Something that disturbed him, made him feel that to enquire into it would be "sticking his neck out."

"Something not for laymen," Dorian said. "Or laywomen, either."

"Probably," Pam said, "something about the man he saw last night at the restaurant." She told Dorian her new theory about Barton Sandford. Which left them, she wanted to know, where?

"Not the aunts," Pam said. "We have to start there. Not Mr. Sandford, because why would the FBI use poison, even if? Not Mrs. Sandford, because she doesn't seem to be around and why? Particularly if he's with the government, because she wouldn't want to embarrass him. It must be difficult enough to be with the government even without cyanide. So we've got the Hickeys and Mrs. Logan's son. You know about them?"

Dorian did; that much Bill had told her.

"The Hickeys, Paul Logan, the typewriter," Pam said, ticking them off on fingers. "You know about the typewriter?"

Dorian did know.

"I still think—" Pam began, but Dorian shook her head. If that had been checked, it had been checked; if the police said there was only one typewriter, there was only one typewriter.

"Probably," Dorian said, "Mrs. Svenson didn't get it straight."

They went then to see Mrs. Rose Hickey, getting

her address by telephone from Hilda Svenson at the Logan house. That, at any rate, Mrs. Svenson did get straight. Mrs. Hickey, plump and round, a woman who should have been surrounded by an aura of comfortableness but today was not, let them in. She said, "The poor dears," about Pamela North's aunts, and what could the police be thinking of?

Pam, taking more words than usual, explained what she and her friend Dorian Hunt were trying to do. Dorian showed no surprise that Pam used her maiden name, which was also the name under which, as a commercial artist, Dorian worked. They had not planned it, but had not needed to.

"We're trying to find something," Pam said, "anything that will help make the police understand my aunts had nothing to do with it. We—well, we just thought you might be able to help."

"Oh," Rose Hickey said, "I do so wish I could. But I've kept going over and over it in my mind and—well, there just isn't anything." She looked at the two younger women. "I just can't believe it," she said. Her eyes filled with tears. "Grace was such a wonderful person," she said. "And to think that our last words were—were harsh!"

Mrs. Logan, Pam suggested, had been worried, upset. Because she was, some little thing had come to seem important. Mrs. Hickey mustn't blame herself.

"She said such dreadful things," Mrs. Hickey said. "That my Lynn was—" But then she stopped and looked at Pam and Dorian uncertainly. "I wasn't going to tell anybody," she said. "And it wouldn't help you, my dear." This last was to Pam.

"Of course not," Pam said. "I realize that. Except—any little thing—Mrs. Logan's state of mind. Mountains out of molehills and that sort of thing. You know?"

From the expression on Mrs. Hickey's face it was not certain that she did.

"To fill out the picture," Dorian said, gently.

"My poor aunts are so—" Pam said, and stopped as if words could not convey the way it was with her poor aunts.

"Well," Mrs. Hickey said, "I don't see how it will help. And—and it's so painful, of course. But—"

It was true that Mrs. Hickey and Mrs. Logan had quarreled—"only it wasn't *really* a quarrel"—about Paul Logan's desire to marry Lynn Hickey. It was true that Mrs. Logan had said unpleasant things about Lynn—"dreadful things, not true at all"—and that Mrs. Hickey, after trying to quieten her friend—"she was so upset, you know"—had herself lost quietness and flared back.

"She said Lynn was hard," Mrs. Hickey said. "Hard and—and mercenary. That she wanted Paul's money, that is, Grace Logan's money, which Paul gets when Grace—" She stopped. "Gets now," she corrected, and again her eyes filled. "That she was a bad influence on Paul, who ought to marry some gentle little thing who wouldn't—" She stopped of her own accord, as if something had on that instant become clear to her. "She said, 'try to change him,' " Rose Hickey said, rather slowly. "Maybe she meant more than that. Maybe without knowing it she meant, 'try to get him out from under my thumb. Untie the apron strings.' " She looked at Pam and Dorian. "I didn't think of that until just now," she said. "Is it an awful thing to think?"

"We can't help what we think," Dorian said. "Perhaps it was true."

"She seemed really to—to almost *hate* Lynn," Mrs. Hickey said. "And Lynn's so sweet, really. Grace said—said dreadful things, finally. I tried not to listen. That there wasn't anything Lynn wouldn't do to—to—"

She stopped. It was as if she had tripped over her own words. Her eyes widened.

"People say such dreadful things when they're excited and upset," Pam North said quickly. "Absurd, angry things, just to hurt people. And poor Mrs. Logan was upset, wasn't she?"

She mustn't think about what she said, Pam thought; mustn't hear her own words again, mustn't think we heard them, or thought they had meaning.

"That's what we really have to find out," Pam said, the words hurrying. "What she was upset about, or afraid of or—didn't she give you any hint, Mrs. Hickey?"

It worked, or seemed to. Mrs. Hickey's face lost its expression of shock. She hesitated, as if giving the question thought.

"Only about Sally," she said. "Sally Sandford, you know? She's left Barton, I'm afraid, and of course that upset Grace, because she's so fond of both of them. It did make her nervous, I think. I don't know of anything else."

"Hilda," Pam said, "Hilda Svenson thought that something had happened in the last few weeks that particularly upset Mrs. Logan. Something connected with Sally. Did you feel that?"

"There may have been," Rose Hickey said. "I'm not sure. Sometimes I felt that Grace confided more in Hilda, really, than she did in me. Of course, Hilda's really a very sympathetic person. You'd never think she—but I mustn't say that."

They waited.

"Only that she has these dreadfully radical ideas," Mrs. Hickey said. "Almost—almost communistic, really." She spoke the dreadful word in a special tone. "It's the way she was brought up, of course. In Europe, you know."

Mrs. Svenson, Pam thought quickly, must have been "brought up," if one could arbitrarily delegate the years from perhaps five to perhaps twenty as those of bringing up, some fifty to thirty-five years before.

"I thought she was Swedish," Dorian said.

"But dear," Mrs. Hickey said, "it's almost as bad in Sweden. Didn't you know? The government *owns*

things. And I myself heard Hilda say, when there was
one of those dreadful strikes—or was going to be, on
the railroads, I think—that the government ought just
to take them over. Without a by your leave or anything," She looked from one to the other of the younger women. "Think of all the people who own stock,"
she said. "Even not very much stock."

They thought for a moment of people who owned
stock, even not very much.

"But she's not *really* a communist?" Pam said.
"Mrs. Svenson, I mean. I mean, not one of the *real*
ones? The Stalin ones?"

"She says not," Mrs. Hickey said. "All the same,
she did say that about the railroads. Or maybe it was
the mines. Of course, maybe she's just confused, a
confused liberal." She paused. "I will say," she admitted, "Hilda said dreadful things about Stalin, too. True
things, of course. But after the railroads, I couldn't
help wondering."

Dorian looked at Pam, her almost green eyes enig-
matical. They had got a long way from the point, Pam
thought. Only, of course, some of the people people
called communists really were. And if Hilda Svenson
really was—

"Didn't you want to ask Mrs. Hickey about the
typewriter, Pam?" Dorian said.

"Oh, of course," Pam said, removing her mind from
the tricky field of espionage into which it had wan-
dered. "About the typewriter—"

She told Mrs. Hickey what Hilda had said about the
typewriter—or had said Mrs. Logan had said about the
typewriter. "Sally's typewriter, I thought," Pam said.

Mrs. Hickey proved as distractable from the subject
of the communist threat as she had been from that of
her daughter. But she was not helpful. She knew that
Sally owned and used, and had for years owned and
used, a portable typewriter, and that she wrote all her
personal letters on it. She had, indeed, been able to
recognize as from Sally Sandford envelopes addressed

to Mrs. Logan because there was "something about them." But Mrs. Logan had said nothing to her to indicate that there had been, lately, anything "wrong" about the typewriter. And she herself had seen no difference in the addresses on letters Mrs. Logan had recently received; they were still obviously from Sally Sandford.

"Your poor aunts," Mrs. Hickey said, reverting from the typewriter, which she clearly considered exhausted as a topic. "It must be so dreadful for them. Such sweet old ladies. Surely they won't actually *arrest* them?"

Pam could only say she hoped not. The aunts were, of course, very worried. They were, she thought, more or less confined to the hotel, in a polite but still firm manner.

Mrs. Hickey had been, she said, always so fond of Pamela's dear aunts, in spite of seeing them so infrequently. She wondered whether it would be all right if she called on them at the hotel. Did Mrs. North think that would be appropriate?

Mrs. North did. She thought it would be very sweet of Mrs. Hickey. She also thought, but did not say, that Mrs. Hickey and Aunt Thelma would find common ground in the perils confronting those who owned stock, even if not very much. The aunts, as a matter of fact, owned a good deal. They could all talk about Mr. Taft.

Leaving, and as if by afterthought, Pam expressed regret that Lynn had not been home and was told that she never, of course, was home during the day. "She goes to business," Mrs. Hickey explained. "She has a very excellent position. A buyer, you know." Pam was interested. Mrs. Hickey gave them the name of the store in which her daughter worked.

"The poor thing," Pam said, as they waved at taxicabs in the street. "I wonder if Mrs. Logan was right about her daughter?"

A cab stopped. Pamela North gave the driver the

name of the store for which Miss Lynn Hickey, who might be hard, might be mercenary, might be a person who would do anything, bought misses' sports wear. She wouldn't have to much longer, Pam thought, and mentioned to Dorian. There was nothing now to stop her marriage to Paul Logan, who apparently was inheriting a pleasant sum of money.

"I know," Dorian said. "We've got to, of course. Because of the aunts and—well, things have got to be found out. All the same—"

"Nobody likes it, Dorian," Pam said. "Somebody has to, all the same. And if everything's all right, then there's nothing wrong, of course. I mean, we don't hurt anybody. Do you know people at this store—Forsyte's?"

Dorian did. She knew the advertising manager, for whom she had done fashion drawings. She also, she thought, knew the head buyer of misses' sports wear—or had a month ago. Buyers, she noted, came and went.

7

It was all very well for dear Thelma to be superior; in almost all matters, and especially in those of real importance, she *was* superior, and Lucinda Whitsett had no thought of questioning a fact so immutable. I *am* the flighty one, Lucinda thought, and was at the same time aware that being the flighty one, the literary one, should embarrass her more than it did, or at least than it always did. It was all very well for Thelma to say "Lucinda!" in that special tone, because certainly such divagations as Lucinda was prone to would be inclined to annoy a no-nonsense person like dear Thelma. (Miss Lucinda Whitsett liked the word "divagations," which she had read somewhere. She often thought it, although it was rather ungainly for speech.)

But all the same, Miss Lucinda thought as she hung up the telephone which had not been answered, it *is* worth looking into, whatever Thelma would think. Even if there is no use in taking it up with Thelma, since she's already snorted at it, and even if dear Pamela isn't home, and dear Gerald not at his office, one can't just sit by and do nothing. That was what had happened in the story she'd read, the story which was really the key to all of this, and the delay which resulted was almost fatal. This time, the delay had already been fatal, if she was right, and might be gain, because poor dear Thelma—

114

If she had only been able to get hold of Pamela, Pamela would have known what to do. Pamela would see at once how probable the whole thing was, once you remembered the story which was a key to every-thing, and would then be able to take, or at any rate to advise, the proper practical steps. Thelma wouldn't listen, already hadn't listened; and Penny—well, Penny just wouldn't *bestir* herself. Particularly as it might mean a trip out of town. It had to have happened out of town because, however ingeniously it had been done, it would by this time have revealed itself if it were a question of the city.

Of course, Miss Lucinda thought at this point, there *is* concrete—or am I thinking of cement?—but that would be so difficult without the proper facilities, whereas in the country it shouldn't really be difficult at all. Once, that is, somebody nerved himself to it, which was in itself incomprehensible. Yet there were more things, as someone had told someone— Horatio?—than are easy to dream of in the everyday philosophy. One can smile and smile and be a villain still, as is vouched for by the same distinguished source. When one came down to it, there really were persons like that awful man in Dickens who always kicked his dog, and ended by killing someone. One had to face it.

It did not occur to Miss Lucinda that she might be called upon to face it in person until some time after she had telephoned Pamela North and got no answer. Then the idea was sudden and unnerving, and at the same time rather fascinating. Of course I *am* flighty, Miss Lucinda thought—and all that. But all the same, Thelma is very, very—well, bossy! Suppose I do read books and remember things in them, is that any reason—?

It wasn't any reason at all, Miss Lucinda decided. Anyway, there was no reason why she should not at least find out whether there was a place in the country where it could have happened, and the way to do that was obviously to look in telephone books. The library, of course, thought Miss Lucinda Whitsett, and at the very thought of a library she brightened. It had been months, it had been last spring, that she had last been in the New York Public Library, where merely being surrounded by so many books made one tingle exquisitely. If nothing else came of it, she would feel all those books around her. Why, one could almost taste them!

There was, of course, the fact that they were not supposed to leave the hotel but, on thinking about it, Miss Lucinda wondered if that really was a fact. Nobody, certainly, had told her, in so many words, that she was not to leave the hotel. Someone might have told Thelma, or even Penny. But no one had told her. One never knew until one tried. "He either fears his fate too much or his deserts are small who fears to put it to the touch, to win or lose it all," Miss Lucinda quoted to herself. With this quotation finished—was it *quite* right, or wasn't it?—Miss Lucinda acted upon it. She opened the door of her room at the Hotel Welby and stepped out into the corridor. Then she thought of something and went back in. She sat at the writing table provided by the hotel and used one of the pens provided by the hotel, this last with difficulty. She read what she had written and was satisfied.

"Gone to the library to find the place. Cripland not Gribland," she had written. If she were delayed—there was always a chance she would be delayed in a library—and either Thelma or Penny came to find her, the one who came would find the note instead, and not be worried.

Miss Lucinda again opened the door of her room and stepped into the corridor. She stepped, briskly for a small, rather frail lady, toward the elevators.

When she reached the elevators, she was joined by a plump, comfortable woman who apparently had come from the other end of the corridor, also, it first appeared, to get on the elevator. But while they waited, the plump comfortable woman spoke, saying "Going out, Miss Whitsett?" and at once Miss Lucinda knew who she was. A policewoman; perhaps even a matron.

"Oh dear no," Miss Lucinda said quickly. "Just down to the lobby for stamps."

The matron, or policewoman, looked pointedly at Miss Lucinda's head, which had a hat on it—a pink hat. At least, the policewoman supposed it was meant to be a hat.

"One always wears a hat," Miss Lucinda said, quickly. "In Cleveland."

The other woman said, "Oh." She said, "They'd rather you didn't leave the hotel, you know."

"Of course," Miss Lucinda said. An elevator stopped then, and she got into it. The other woman did not, although for a moment she hesitated. She was not supposed to do more than, by her presence, by words if necessary, remind the Misses Whitsett of their tacit detention. (If necessary, she might go further with Miss Thelma Whitsett.) The ladies were not expected to lam out; if they did they could quickly be retrieved. In any case, the one who had just gone for stamps was the littlest, and most fluttery. She would not go far. Of course, if she tried to, steps might be taken.

Miss Lucinda, who liked to be as truthful as circumstances permitted, did stop at the hotel desk and did buy stamps, although she did not really need them. But then, with the air of an elderly lady going out for a breath of air, Miss Lucinda went out of the hotel and walked toward Fifth Avenue. She walked sedately, but this was not a manner assumed. She was always sedate, even if a little flighty. She looked about her with great interest in everything, and this, also, she always did.

At Fifth, which was only a little over a block from the hotel, she took a Fifth Avenue bus northward, although the library was then only a few blocks away. She took the bus because she had always enjoyed Fifth Avenue buses when she was in New York—and because, although she had learned better a year before, she still kept thinking that Fifth Avenue buses, unlike other buses, *had* to provide enough seats to go around. The one she got onto did not.

She got off at Fortieth Street, waited for the lights to change, and crossed the street to the library. She went between the lions and up the broad stairs.

At the desk inside, she enquired the whereabouts of out-of-town telephone directories and was instructed. She started with areas in New York State, although realizing that she might have, in the end, to go on to Connecticut or even New Jersey. But, as it happened, she did not. She found what she wanted very quickly and made a memorandum, since what she wrote down she always remembered.

It was so easy, indeed, that Miss Lucinda could only believe she was being guided. It was with that in mind that she decided on her next step.

Miss Lynn Hickey was not at Forsyte's; an assistant buyer, she was out assistant buying. She was, however, expected back in an hour or so. Pam and Dorian, being in misses' sports wear, decided to pass the time, assisted by Dorian's acquaintance, the senior buyer, who was still there but God knew for how long. There was a delightful sweater-skirt ensemble in a kind of dusty brown which was perfect for Dorian—ideal, as Pam pointed out, for a long walk in the country, if Dorian ever wanted one. Pam herself found almost nothing, except one or two things in the going-to-Florida-line which would be perfect for next summer; things much better than would be available for next summer next spring. "Because," Pam pointed out, saying charge and send, "it's always the winter summer people who get the best of everything." (It turned out subsequently that Pam had no charge account at Forsyte's, but Forsyte's happily opened one for her and sent the one or two things—a slacks and shirt outfit and a play suit which would, Dorian remarked, make almost any man want to play.)

The interlude, almost pastoral in its gay-hearted simplicity, was ended by the return of Miss Lynn Hickey, who was five feet and perhaps ninety-five pounds of directed vigor; who was extremely pretty in a somewhat businesslike manner and who was, beyond any doubt, brisk. One would have thought her older than she probably was until, when she remembered Pam North, she said, "Oh" and for an instant appeared younger than she probably was. The manner might be office-hours deep, Pam thought, and explained about her aunts and their predicament, and asked help.

"I'm so sorry," she said to Pamela, her office-hours manner back again, and, to the senior buyer, "The Frankleberg line stinks, for my money. There might be one or two things."

"I don't see how I can help," she said to Pamela, when her demolition of the Frankleberg line had been acknowledged.

"I am terribly sorry about your aunts, and about Paul's poor mother, but—"

She shrugged her shoulders, which were as trim as the rest of her.

Pamela realized all that. She was clutching at straws. "Leaving no stone unturned," she added.

"You see," Dorian Weigand, who was still Dorian Hunt for the day, said gravely, "Pam feels that there's always a needle in every haystack."

Miss Hickey was crisply amused and the others laughed pleasantly with her.

"So often," Pam said, "people really don't remember what they *do* remember. I thought you—couldn't you have lunch with us?"

Lynn looked doubtful. "Of couse she can," her senior said. "Well—" Lynn said. "Some place that won't take too long. There's a Schrafft's across the street."

There was and it was not yet crowded. The hostess

was as serene as a ship in a light breeze; the waitress, when she arrived, was panting like a tugboat in her haste or, perhaps, in anticipation of labors to come. Lynn refused a cocktail at first, then relented. They sipped, ladylike in ladylike surroundings, two of them looking for a murderer.

"We hoped—" Pam began, and then Lynn Hickey leaned toward her, her eyes bright, her face serious.

"I may as well tell you," she said, "mother telephone me after you talked to her. The poor dear."

Pam North said, "Oh."

"She wasn't very clear," Lynn said. "She often isn't. Older people so often aren't, are they?" She looked intently at Pam, who realized that she was, after all, older than Lynn. As, she told herself, most people were. It was nevertheless startling to be, even by the implication of a glance, associated with Lynn's mother.

"I'm afraid," Lynn said, "she may have given you a false impression. I did not kill Paul's mother." She smiled, superficially. "But of course I'd say that, wouldn't I?"

"Yes," Pam said. "You would, wouldn't you?"

"And Paul didn't," Lynn said. She was decisive. It occurred to Pamela that she was, on the whole, too decisive.

"Then," Pam said, "there isn't any reason to be so afraid, is there? So keyed up?"

The girl suddenly finished the rest of her drink. She looked into the glass; she put in slim fingers and extracted the olive, and looked at it and then ate it. Little Jill Horner, Pam thought. Or am I just supposed to think that?

"All right," Lynn said, looking again at Pam, looking then at Dorian. "I'm keyed up. My mother quarrels with somebody, because the somebody says— well, makes accusations against me. Paul and I want to get married and his mother doesn't want us to. Wants to keep dear little Paul under her dear, god-damned little thumb. And she gets killed. Now we can get married; Paul gets a lot of money; I quit my job. We live happily ever after. Where—in Sing Sing?"

She lifted the empty glass as if to drink from it; put it down again, too hard.

"Or we have nice electric easy chairs side by side," she said. "In front of the fire. On the fire. We—"

She looked up suddenly.

"They said you'd probably be here," Paul Logan said. "You're all keyed up, kid."

"Damn," Lynn Hickey said. "Oh—*damn!*"

"Anyway," Paul Logan said, "what business is it of yours, Mrs. North? Or of this lady's?" He indicated Dorian.

"Dorian Hunt," Pamela said. "This is Mr. Logan. Won't you sit down, Mr. Logan? We haven't accused your—Miss Hickey, of anything. IGm trying to help my Aunt Thelma." But then she looked from one to the other. "And," she said, "I will."

She wasn't doing it now, Paul Logan said, but he sat down.

"Won't you have a drink?" Pamela North said, polite in fury. Not, she thought, that they didn't have a right to be furious too, if you came to that. Or, on the other hand, frightened.

Nothing, she realized, ever stayed at a pitch. Now there was the business of trying to attract the waitress, who was doing nothing in particular with a kind of furious intentness; who, finally attracted, panted anxiously to them; who panted away again and was then, for minutes, always so much an impending event that nothing which she might interrupt could be begun. Pamela heard herself remarking on the remarkable lingering of summer in the lap of fall. This was politely noticed by the others. The waitress panted back in triumph, put down a cocktail and spilled part of it.

"All I'm—" Pam began.

"Would you care to order?" the waitress enquired, with intense good will.

"We—" Paul Logan began, his delicately handsome face reddening. But then he smiled suddenly and spread his hands in surrender. They ordered. The waitress panted off.

"Since we've all got the chips off," Pam said, "Dorian and I are just trying to find out what people remember. So—"

That Mrs. Logan had opposed their marriage, neither of them denied. When they talked of that, the girl was very young again. She kept looking at Paul as if, however she tried, she must continually reassure herself of his presence. Of the two, now, he was the more assured. Lynn's mother and Paul's had quarreled over something Mrs. Logan had charged against Lynn. They did not phrase the charge, or need to. They had no idea who else might have wanted Mrs. Logan dead, and when they spoke of his mother, Paul's lips were stiff by obvious effort. And Paul, who might have, denied knowing anything about a wrong typewriter, or about Sally, except that she could not be found.

"But," he said, "she can't have anything to do with it. She left—oh, weeks ago. Before we came back to town after Labor Day."

"Back to town?" Pam said.

Paul and his mother had spent most of August at a summer place they had—"not much more than a cabin, really"—near Patterson, New York. Sally and Barton Sandford had spent his vacation, also during August, in a similar place a couple of hundred yards away. Paul and the Sandfords had played tennis at a near-by club; they had had, and made, use of a swimming pool on the estate of some friends of Mrs. Logan's. It had been a pleasant, relaxed month.

But during it, it now appeared, something had arisen between the Sandfords. Neither Paul nor his mother had noticed anything; on Labor Day itself they had all been at the pool, with a good many others, and the

Sandfords had seemed as always. Two days later, Sandford had come around to the Logan house in town, his face set, to tell Mrs. Logan that her niece had left him, for reasons he insisted he did not know. They had, he said, planned to drive in to New York Tuesday morning. But instead, Sally, who was driving, had taken them to the railroad station at Brewster.

And there, in the car, parked in front of the station, she had, Sandford said, told him she was not going back to town—that she was going—that she didn't know where she was going. Some place to "think things out." He had been, he told Mrs. Logan, utterly surprised and bewildered; he had been so taken aback that he had not known how to argue with her.

"He said," Paul remembered, "that it was 'too damn intangible to talk about.' That's what mother told me; I stayed on in the country the rest of the week. Heard about it when I got back."

In the end Sandford had taken the train. He thought he had got from Sally a half promise to reconsider; he had expected her, in the end, to drive home to town. But she had not.

"But what has that to do with—with what happened to mother?" Paul said. "What—"

The waitress panted up with their food, including several items they had not ordered. They hung in air while she presented, triumphantly, the provender she had intrepidly snatched, one could only assume, from enraged cooks. She rearranged all the little paper doilies. Finally, she panted off.

But now Paul Logan merely sat and looked at his food. The others waited.

"If Sally had had any reason to want—to want to harm mother," he said slowly, "you could work out something. She goes away, ostensibly out west somewhere. She's gone at the time the poison was put in the medicine bottle. Presumably. So—she's the only one who, apparently, couldn't have put it there. I could have, Lynn could have, Bart—Hilda—Lynn's mother even. But not Sally. If—*she really did go that far.*"

"The letters," Pam told him. "The letters your mother got."

"Perhaps she could have got—oh, somebody, to mail them for her," he said. "I don't know—there'd be ways of doing things like that. She could even go places in airplanes and mail them herself, I suppose. She could actually be living here in New York somewhere, she could have—" He stopped suddenly. "She had a key to the house," he said. "At least, she always had had. I don't think she ever gave it back."

There aren't, Pam thought, really any flaws in it. It could have been that way. But—

"Why?" Pam said. "Why would she want to—to kill your mother?"

"I don't—" Paul began and stopped. "There's always money," he said. "Mother's money. Sally gets quite a bit of it."

"Fifty thousand, wasn't it?" Pam asked, and Logan thought so.

"A lot, of course," Pam said, "but still, not very much. Unless you need it dreadfully. Do they? I thought Sally had money herself?"

"Sally?" Paul said. "I don't think so. A few thousand, maybe. Not very much." He looked, with puzzled eyes, at the chicken hash on his plate; he said he was trying to remember something. He couldn't, he said, make it come clear. It was something about—he snapped his fingers.

"Bart's worked out something, he said. A—a medicine or something. A formula. Wanted to make it; wanted a laboratory of his own. I remember that." He paused, snapped his fingers again. "Asked mother early in the summer if she didn't want to put some money in it," Paul said. "Said it would be a gold mine. Half joking, you know, but meaning it all the same. Mother—mother said she didn't believe in gold mines."

Whether Barton Sandford had, later, made his request more formally, not half jokingly, Paul didn't know. His mother had not mentioned it to him. But he was certain Sandford had not, if he asked for money, got it.

"All the same," Paul said, "I know—I'm sure—Sal's all right."

"You're an innocent," Lynn said. "A babe in arms. You think everybody's all right."

He looked at her; he seemed puzzled and uncertain.

"I don't think so," he said. "Am I, Lynn?"

"It's all right," she said. "It's a fine way to be. If there's somebody—" She broke off short.

"I'm sorry, Lynn," he said, and the others might not have been there.

"Nobody wants you to change," Lynn told him. "Hear me? Nobody. It was never that."

He looked at her.

"Oh," she said, "you believe everybody, don't you? Everybody but me." She became, then, conscious of the others. She said she was sorry. She said, trying to be on top of it, trying to be crisp, that everything was coming out, that she was a sieve.

"About Mrs. Sandford," Pam said. "You don't agree with Mr. Logan?"

Lynn Hickey hesitated a moment. She extracted lettuce from a chicken sandwich and looked to see whether anything remained. Then she said Sally was all right. She said Sally was a fine person. Her tone put the tribute in capital letters, and so diminished it.

"The salt of the earth," Lynn said. "With such a wonderful, wonderful conscience. Such a—a righteous person." Lynn seemed surprised at the unfamiliar word, but then approved it. "Righteous," she said. "That's it. Never easygoing, with herself or anybody. This business of 'thinking things out.' Whoever 'thinks things out'? That way, I mean. The kind of things I suppose she's thinking out? About herself and Bart?"

She looked suddenly at Pam North. The she looked at Dorian.

"You don't," she said. "Neither of you does. It—it makes people all stiff inside. But Sally—well, she'd wonder, all at once, whether she was worthy of Bart, or he was worthy of her, or something. Whether their life together was really *right*. She'd have to Get Things Straightened Out."

She looked at Pam again.

"Does anybody, ever?" she asked.

"Not that way," Pam said. "At least, I never do. But then, I just never think of it."

That was it, Lynn said. That was precisely it. Sally Sandford did.

"A sense of duty," Dorian suggested, and Lynn said, "God yes!

"However," she said then, "that doesn't fit with her—her killing anybody, does it?"

It didn't, apparently. They agreed it didn't. But then, after a pause, during which they ate, Pam North said, "Still—

"It can lead to the end justifying the means," she said. "One sacrificed for—for many, I guess. If Mr. Sandford had found out something which would save millions of people, and Mrs. Logan stood in the way—I mean, not having her fifty thousand stood in the way—a very conscientious person might—" She paused. "It might seem like a kind of mathematics," she said. "Adding and subtracting. Not—not people at all. Like dictatorships," she said. She looked at the others. Paul Logan shook his head and then Dorian Weigand smiled faintly.

"Or," she said, "it might be merely wanting fifty thousand dollars. Because it would be fun to have, and to spend. That would be simpler, wouldn't it? Particularly if you didn't have very much and wanted to get free from something and start over."

"I don't think Sally—" Paul Logan began, and then

stopped abruptly. "Or aren't you talking about Sally?" he asked.

"Oh, about Mrs. Sandford," Dorian said. "I thought Pam was making it a little complicated."

Paul Logan looked at Dorian as if waiting for her to go on, but she merely shook her head and said that that was all. But the fact that, by implication, it was not all hung in the air. Paul Logan had got money too by his mother's death, and freedom too. Freedom, among other things, to marry Lynn Hickey—Lynn who had been, by the woman now dead, characterized as up to anything; Lynn who had herself characterized Sally Sandford as a woman who might be hardened by righteousness.

"I suppose," Pam North said, "that somebody made sure Mrs. Sandford hadn't merely gone back to the country place? But of course, somebody did?"

That, of course, had been done. By Sandford himself, the Wednesday after Labor Day. And, a few days later, by Paul who, being at the Logan cottage, had walked over to the Sandfords' and found it locked and empty, cleaned up and closed up for the winter. Having said this, Logan looked from Pam to Dorian, waiting politely, letting show the faint impatience of one who feels a topic exhausted. Lynn Hickey looked at her watch, obviously, and then at Pamela. Her expression said "Well?"

I'm not being good at this, Pam thought; I'm not getting anything except things all along obvious—that Lynn and Paul Logan are in love and want to get married, that now they can, that they had pointed, not too subtly, to Sally Sandford. We are, Pam North, thought, precisely where we were when we came in. She picked up gloves and bag; she tried to attract the waitress.

The waitress, who before had seemed omnipresent, seemed to hang constantly over them, panting, now did not attract. She was around. She puffed up to a near-by table with a glass of water and looked full at Pam and did not see her and puffed off again. She panted back and Pam said, "Oh, waitress!" and the waitress did not hear. She puffed away, prodigiously harassed. Pam watched her go and sighed. She tried to attract a serenely floating hostess, but the hostess floated incased in impervious transparency. Pam said, "Oh *dear*."

"Let me get it," Paul said. "You two go on. If—"

Pam couldn't think of it. She had brought about the whole, apparently pointless, incident. She could at least pay for it. She saw the waitress again and waved anxiously. The waitress looked at her blankly and Pam realized it was another waitress. Perhaps if she stood up—

She started to and the waitress, who had been hiding—*must* have been hiding—swooped upon them. She swooped indignantly, as if finally, at too long last, unconscionable lingerers showed signs of movement. She had the bill ready and thrust it upon Logan, who promptly put it in one pocket and produced change from another. Even that hadn't worked, Pam thought, making the best of it. She couldn't get information; she couldn't even get to pay for the food. She stood up, and everybody else stood up. By agreement, they made suitable sounds of separation at the table; Lynn and Paul Logan were thanked for their patience; they, in turn, were sorry they had not helped.

Lynn and Paul went first, as behooved check payers. They paid and passed on, Dorian and Pam behind them—close behind them; closer, it appeared, than Paul Logan realized.

"—that damned typewriter," Paul said to Lynn. "I don't see how we missed—"

Then Lynn went into a segment of a revolving door and Paul stopped. He took the next segment.

Little Miss Lucinda went down the stairs in the Grand Central Terminal with one hand lightly on the handrail. Marble stairs were so treacherous. People hurried past her and some of them seemed impatient, although she was taking up very little room. At the bottom of the stairs she discovered she had soiled the fingers of a glove and thought how unlike Cleveland everything was in New York. She went to the information kiosk and made enquiry—she had mislaid the memorandum, but that did not matter, since she did not forget anything once she had written it down. She was given a diminutive timetable.

Timetables were no trouble for Miss Lucinda, since they were designed to be read. On the trip east, indeed, she had read extensively in a much larger timetable, having exhausted other reading matter. She had, with interest, discovered on which trains baggage could not be checked, which did not run on Saturdays and Sundays and Holiday A, which were "Pullmans Only" and which were not. She found especially interesting the listings of equipment on various through trains—"diner Albany to New York," "buffet lounge New York to Chicago," "reduced fare tickets not honored on this train." She was interested in these things, not for any practical reason, not even because she was especially fond of trains, but because the information had been written out and printed. For the same reason, she often read entirely through the extended directions which sometimes came with patent medicines, and, when there were translations, read the French version as well and did what she could with German. Miss Lucinda liked to read.

So she had no trouble whatever with the simple tables of the Harlem Division of the New York Central Railroad; at eleven forty-five she discovered that a Pawling local left at one forty-six. She bought herself several things to read on the trip and then had lunch in the Commodore Grill, finding it unexpectedly full of men, all of whom were drinking. Emboldened by example, Miss Lucinda had a sherry while she waited for her luncheon to be served, and read the *Atlantic*

Monthly. She finished luncheon in too ample time, went to the newsreel theater and then went looking for her train.

The gates were not yet open when she reached them, and then she debated whether, after all, it would not be the right thing to telephone Thelma, or at any rate Penny—better Penny, on the whole—and explain what she was doing. Because, Miss Lucinda thought, while my note was perfectly clear, they might not quite understand and might worry. She became almost sure she ought to do this, and had even turned away to look for a telephone booth, when she realized clearly what would happen. She would get Thelma, even if she got Penny first, and Thelma would say "Lucinda!" in that certain tone. And then, Miss Lucinda knew, she would give the whole thing up, since there was no use pretending she had an answer to "Lucinda!" said in the certain tone. And she did not want to give the whole thing up; because now, in addition to feeling that she was being guided, she had begun to feel that she was having a very exciting time. It might, she realized, be partly the sherry, but it was nevertheless exciting.

Why, Miss Lucinda thought to herself, it's almost like something one reads about.

And, in addition, she was really doing it for Thelma, against whom such ridiculous charges were being, or almost being, made. There was always that; it was really her duty not to let herself be stopped. It was really—

Then the gates were opened and Miss Lucinda, with fifteen or twenty other early comers, went through them, and down a long ramp and then along a platform walled on either side by unlighted railroad coaches. They must, Miss Lucinda thought, have walked half a dozen blocks before they finally came to the lighted coaches—four of them—of the Pawling local. They were very old coaches and had the gritting feeling of very old coaches. There were plenty of uncomfortable seats. Miss Lucinda got one and found her ticket and held it in her hand ready—she hated to have to scramble through her bag at the last moment, the way so many women did—and resumed her reading of the *Atlantic Monthly*.

Looking at her, no one could have dreamed the kind of trip upon which Miss Lucinda had embarked or what she expected to find at the end of it.

There was no need, when Pam and Dorian stood on the sidewalk in front of Schrafft's, expelled in turn by the revolving door, for Pam to ask Dorian whether she had heard what Paul Logan had said. So Pam said, "Well, what do you think of that? He *does* know something about the typewriter. So Sally *is* in it."

"She always was, I think," Dorian said, and said then, "There they are."

Paul Logan and Lynn were walking toward Fifth Avenue. They were obviously talking intently. It appeared that, of the two, Lynn was talking the more. Without consultation, Pam and Dorian turned also toward Fifth Avenue.

"Maybe," Pam said, "they'll do something about something. Which side of the street do you want?"

Dorian blinked the lids over greenish eyes.

"We stick out," Pam said. "If we're going to tail, we ought to separate. At least on other sides of the street. Or would that be more conspicuous?"

It would, if they were seen at all, be much more conspicuous, Dorian thought. The two of them advancing along opposite sidewalks in pursuit of prey would, if noticed by Paul and Lynn, hardly fail to arouse their interest. Pam and Dorian, therefore, stayed together.

"If they split up, we will," Pam told Dorian, who agreed, but said, "What will they do something about?"

"The typewriter," Pam said. "Sally. Because

they've remembered something, only—" She broke off completely, and looked puzzled.

"Right," Dorian Weigand said. "I can't see we're getting anywhere. Who do you suspect?"

"Everybody," Pam said, hopelessly. "Except the aunts, of course. Mrs. Sandford most, I guess. But that girl knows something, and so does he. About the typewriter, probably. And Mrs. Logan did too, and perhaps that was why—they're turning uptown."

Paul Logan and Lynn Hickey, still talking, were the ones turning uptown. They crossed the street and went north on Fifth. Pam and Dorian increased their saunter to something nearer a trot, reached the intersection, dodged turning taxicabs and went after them. They quickly got too close, and sauntered again. Then, midway of the block, Paul and Lynn stopped in front of Forsyte's.

"We're too close," Pam said, "we'll have to look in windows."

They veered toward windows, bumping their way among south-bound pedestrians. The window they reached was dedicated to the wares of the Forsyte Men's Shop.

"The trouble with tailing," Pam said, "is that you never get the right window. Or being tailed, for that matter. Can you see them, without looking?"

Dorian could. Paul and Lynn were standing in front of the Forsyte entrance, still talking. Dorian thought he was suggesting something of which the girl was doubtful, since she looked doubtful and shook her head.

"She's nodding now," Dorian reported to Pam, who was looking with rather ostentatious innocence at a tweed suit—again nothing Jerry would approve. Pam, whose theory had been that two looks are four times as suspicious as one, abandoned the tweed suit.

Lynn Hickey made a small flicking motion with her right hand and went suddenly into Forsyte's. Paul stood for a moment. Then he walked unhesitatingly to Pam and Dorian.

"Can't I drop you some place?" he enquired.

"Drop us?" Pam said, feeling as if he already had. "Oh—thanks no, Mr. Logan. You go right ahead about whatever you're—I mean, we're just window-shopping."

Paul looked at the window; he said, "Oh." He said, "All right then," turned away quickly and, seemingly in the same movement, was engulfed by a taxicab which had just discharged. The cab started south and was, almost at once, stopped in traffic.

Pam tugged Dorian's sleeve and they bumped among south- and north-bound pedestrians to the curb. A cab swerved to them. Pam led the way. She said what she had always wanted to say.

"Follow that cab!" Pamela North commanded.

The driver, who had already knocked down the meter flag, leaned toward them. He said, "Huh, lady?"

"That cab," Pam said. "Follow it." She pointed. The cab in question began to move off.

"You a cop?" the driver said. "A lady cop? Or something?"

"No but—" Pam said.

"Then it's no, lady," the cab driver said. "Not me. I'm a married man, see? I got three children, see? I—"

"It hasn't anything to do with your children," Pam told him.

That was, the driver told her, what she said.

"A man's got to decide about his own children," he told her. "If you were a cop, now. As it is, not me, lady."

"This is the most ridiculous thing—" Pam said, but Dorian patted her arm gently.

"The other cab's gone now," Dorian said. "It made a right turn."

"See, lady," the driver said. "Listen to your friend. Take you any other place, lady?"

But that Pamela North wouldn't have. If this were the last cab in New York, it would take her no place. She and Dorian got out. Getting out, Pam looked at the meter, which showed fifteen cents. "The drop's on the clock, lady," the driver told her.

Pamela North did not hesitate. She gave the driver a quarter, and waved off change. It was not until several minutes later that she realized she had paid fifteen cents for sitting in one place, and ten cents, presumably, for discovering that a cab driver had three children.

"I had no idea it was so difficult to trail people," Pam told Dorian. "What should we do now?"

Suddenly both of them stopped walking and faced each other and began to laugh. When they had laughed, Pamela said they might as well go and see how the aunts were coming. Thinking of the aunts, Pam was serious again.

"The poor helpless things," Pam said, and she and Dorian began to walk toward the Welby in the Murray Hill district.

The train ran beautifully for almost half an hour; it was not comfortable, it bumped a good deal, but it went rapidly and with determination. Miss Lucinda read all of a short story in the *Atlantic* and liked it very much. It was a gentle story. When she was reading, Miss Lucinda could forget almost anything, and now she could even forget her errand.

But after this fine start, the train lost impetus. It stopped at White Plains, went on reluctantly for a very short distance and stopped again. This time it stopped at what was, Miss Lucinda discovered by looking at signs, North White Plains. Having got this far, the train seemed entirely to lose interest. Looking up the corridor from the middle of the second, non-smoking, coach, Miss Lucinda discovered that it also lost its locomotive. But the sign had said Pawling.

After another considerable time, however, a steam locomotive backed slowly down the track toward the train. Miss Lucinda watched, fascinated and a little frightened, with the feeling that something surely had gone wrong. The locomotive came on, ever more slowly, as if disgruntled by its approaching task, and just before it hit almost stopped. Miss Lucinda closed her eyes, and there was a jolt. There was then another longish pause, and men walked up and down beside the train. Then, with an even more pronounced jolt, the train started off. It did not go rapidly, now, or with assurance. It went on only for about five minutes and then stopped again.

Toilsomely, then, it progressed toward Pawling, its laborious progress so distracting that not even the *Atlantic* could fully engross Miss Lucinda. Something of the train's obvious disinclination to reach its destination found an echo in Miss Lucinda's mind. Perhaps, she thought , she had been too precipitate, after all.

She also began to think that perhaps she had been wrong. She began, indeed, very much to hope she had been wrong. If it had not been an action so—so fluttery—so much in the character she knew Thelma ascribed to her, Miss Lucinda might have got off the train at Mount Kisco. But she did not.

"If you can convince us there's a tie-in, we'll coöperate," the man on the other side of the desk told Bill Weigand. "We always do. You know that. The trouble is, you're merely playing a hunch."

"Right," Bill told him.

"And when you come down to it," the other man said, "it's an unofficial hunch. Your inspector's satisfied. The county district attorney's satisfied."

"It won't hold," Bill told him.

The man across the desk shrugged, indicating that whether it would hold was a matter on which he had no opinion, and one outside his range of interest.

"It's at a delicate point," the man behind the desk

said then. "It's no reflection on you—certainly not on you. No reflection on any of your people. But we don't want a mob scene."

"I don't," Bill told him, "see precisely how you're going to avoid it, in the end. After the inspector gets through following his red herring. He will, you know."

Again the man shrugged. He said maybe it would all be wound up by then.

"Try this one," Bill said. "Your man's been in and out of the city a good deal recently? In line of duty?"

The man hesitated. Then he said they all got around a good deal on a job like this.

"Right," Bill said. "About your first tip-off. Was it from one of your regular sources?"

The man behind the desk hesitated even longer over that. Then he said, "No comment."

"Or closer home?" Bill said, as if finishing what he had only begun to say.

"Nope," the man said. "Sorry, Weigand. No comment."

Bill waited.

"It's no good," the man told him. "If it were just this one thing, maybe. But there are all sorts of tie-ins in things like this—here, there, everywhere. Damn it, I haven't authority to take a chance on the whole operation, even if I wanted to. You can see that."

"Right," Bill said. He stood up.

"It's a damn nuisance all around," the other man said, standing up too.

Murder usually was, Bill told him. They shook hands. Bill started toward the door; seemed to think of something more.

"Heard from the one who tipped you off recently?" Bill asked.

"Not for—" the other man began, smiled slightly, and finished, "No comment." But then he added, "No reason why we should, you know."

"Right," Bill said. "No reason at all. As a matter of fact, I didn't think you had."

Bill went, then, leaving the other man to look for a moment doubtfully at his closed office door. Then he picked up a telephone and told the answerer to send Saul in.

Bill Weigand retrieved his Buick, parked in a side street off Foley Square, and drove up Lafayette Street. It was still only a hunch; there was nothing much to go on. Nor was there, he thought, at the moment any place to go, except home. He went home.

He expected to find Dorian, and did not. He found a note saying she was out with Pam.

He reached toward the telephone, but it rang under his hand. He listened.

"I thought it would," he said, after listening for more than a minute. He listened again, smiling faintly. "Right," he said. "I'm on my way, Inspector."

He replaced the receiver and wrote a note for Dorian. He wrote, "It blew up in Arty's face. You and Pam keep out of trouble."

He went down in the elevator and was surprised to hear himself whistling. He drove downtown to his office in the West Twentieth Street station.

8

Tuesday, 2:45 P.M. to 4:15 P.M.

"Not *again*," Pam North said. "This is getting to be ridiculous."

All the same, Dorian said, there was a man. There had been for several blocks. If he was not following them, it was a very interesting coincidence. He was a tall man, sauntering on a pleasant afternoon. But wherever they went, he sauntered after.

"After all," Pam said, "we're walking down Madison Avenue. Lots of people do. Of course, we can always stop at a window." She turned toward one, and said, "I'm getting sort of tired or looking in windows. Particularly such—"

She had taken the opportunity to glance back up Madison.

"For heaven's sake," she said. "Look hard, Dorian. It's Mr. Sandford. He's—"

But then, smiling with evident pleasure, Mr. Sandford turned toward them.

"Thought I saw someone familiar," he said. "Said to myself, 'Mrs. North.' Been trying to catch up."

Pamela North said, "Oh." She said that this was Miss Hunt. Everyone was delighted.

But then Barton Sandford's pleasure at the meeting seemed to drain away, and he became serious; worried. He said he understood the police still suspected one of Mrs. North's aunts. He made sounds which deprecated this situation.

138

"We're trying to do something," Pam told him. "But we're not getting anywhere. We thought you were following us."

"Following you?" he repeated. "For God's sake why?" He smiled. "In addition to the obvious reasons, of course," he said.

"Because you're FBI," Pam wanted to say, but thought that she should not, since it would of course embarrass him. She said she didn't know why.

"Except we were trying to follow Paul Logan," she said, "and made a mess of it. I suppose it put the idea in our heads."

Sandford looked at them and shook his own head.

"Because," Pam said, "we thought he knew something about your wife's typewriter."

She explained, in part. She did not mention the suspicion Paul Logan had indicated feeling of Sally Sandford; she did ask whether Sandford was sure his wife was not at the country cottage. He had looked, she understood, and to this he nodded. But could Sally have, in any way, seen him coming—or known he was coming—and hidden until he left? He started to shake his head but then hesitated. What Pam suggested was, of course, possible.

"You suspect her too?" he said, and it was Pam's turn to hesitate. She was about to say again that, still, she suspected everybody, and realized suddenly that that was not true. She suspected two more than the rest—Lynn Hickey, Sally Sandford. "You do," Barton Sandford told her, when she still did not speak. He looked at her with eyes a little narrowed as if, so, he could see more readily into her mind. He said, "I'd hoped—" and broke it off. He pointed out, then, that they couldn't talk there. He suggested he buy them a drink in a place where talk would be possible.

They found a place, uncrowded in this interlude between late lunch and early cocktails. Dorian and Pam sat on a banquette, with Sandford on a chair opposite them. After the drinks came he said, "Why Sally? Not only you. Everybody. Not coming out and saying so. The district attorney, this inspector whatever his name is. Everybody."

"Not those two," Pam told him. "They think my aunt."

Sandford said that, two hours ago, they hadn't acted like it. They had called him for questioning and most of the questioning had been about his wife. Was she—were they—in urgent need of the money Sally would inherit? What had been her attitude toward her aunt? And, as Mrs. North had just asked, was he certain she had not merely stayed in the country cottage, a scant two hours' drive from New York? Didn't he—this a question many times repeated—actually know where she was? Wasn't he lying to protect her? (This last more indirectly phrased.) And that he had been aware of the further implications, although now he did not directly phrase them, was apparent from his attitude and his choice of words—had he and his wife not conspired to kill, for fifty thousand dollars? But the district attorney's assistant had been polite, and had questioned politely. There had been no open suggestion that Sandford was himself under suspicion.

"Did they ask about your discovery," Dorian asked him. "Invention, formula, whatever it was?"

He looked from one to the other of them and reddened slowly. He said, "Oh, you've found that out. Logan, I suppose?"

They did not deny it.

He had not told at the district attorney's office about that. He supposed they would find it out and make a lot of it. There wasn't, he said, a lot to it. There was a formula, yes. It was too complicated to go into, and too technical. He thought it would have a certain usefulness in a certain field; he would like a laboratory in which to manufacture.

"Sally built it up in her own mind," he said. "She—" Then he stopped abruptly, apparently disconcerted by what he had said. "She wouldn't have done anything," he said, after a moment. "I—I know she wouldn't have." But he did not sound assured.

"All the same," Pam pointed out, "you didn't tell the district attorney's people about it."

He hesitated more lengthily this time. Then he shook his head slowly, and by his attitude admitted an implication Pam North had left in her words.

"Sally—Sally's a funny girl," he said, finally. "To hear her talk you'd think—oh, a hell of a lot of things. That she could be ruthless for what she thought was important, was right. You remember when the fascists were teaching children to spy on their parents? Well—Sally didn't defend it. But because she thought the fascists were wrong, not because the thing in itself would be wrong. She'd let people think that, if the fascists had been right, then betrayal of anybody for them would have been right. Of course, she didn't really mean that. I know she didn't."

And again the reiteration of certainty lessened conviction.

It was true, he said—and now he talked without prompting, as if doubts and fears had long been bottled up and now poured out—it was true that she had been urgent that he try again to borrow from Grace Logan enough to get his laboratory equipped and started; it was true that the fifty thousand dollars she would inherit would have given them the start. It was true that much of the last night they had spent together she had argued this, and that his refusal again to apply to her aunt had seemed—

"Well," Barton Sandford said, "it seemed to make her contemptuous of me. She talked about my being 'ineffective,' not having any 'decision of character.' Maybe she was right."

He didn't, Pam thought, seem to realize he was talking to people he hardly knew. He was, she decided, talking to himself; arguing with himself against a possibility which had perhaps tormented him since

Grace Logan died and now, during his questioning at the district attorney's office, had been forced to the front of his mind.

"You'd have thought everything hung on this formula of mine," he said. "The whole damn future of everything. Believe me, it doesn't. I kept telling her that."

But she hadn't accepted that, had taken his disclaimers, it appeared, as merely further evidences of his lack of decisiveness of character. He had supposed, when the next day she would not return to town with him, that it was because she had, in view of her new—or newly confirmed—belief in his inadequacy, to, as she said, "think out" their future. He still thought that; he still thought she had gone off, as all the evidence showed she had, in the car to drive and, presumably, think.

"I'm damned sure of it," he said, but again the tone did not match the words.

"Wherever she is, the typewriter is too," Pam pointed out. "Since we know it's the right typewriter. If she's at the cottage, the typewriter is. Did you look for it when you looked for her?"

He hadn't, specifically. He thought he would have seen it, and realized its importance, if it had been openly in sight. But it might have been anywhere—in a closet, under a table—and he would not have noticed. In a word, no—he hadn't looked for the typewriter; he didn't know it wasn't there.

The return to a matter so specific as the typewriter apparently aroused Barton Sandford to his own loquacity. He said he had been talking too damn much; he apologized. He said he was keyed up. He suggested further drinks.

"I've got to go to the aunts," Pam North said and added, to her own surprise, "I'm a sluggard." She must, she decided, adopt a broader "a," even in her own mind.

Barton Sandford paid for their drinks. It was exasperating, Pamela North thought, that when men want to pay, waiters appear with bills. Sandford said he didn't think Pam needed to worry about her aunts. He thought, he had gathered distinctly, that they now were out of it.

He walked with them down Madison for a few more blocks, then went off east, apologizing once more for, he said, "having talked their ears off." They went on to the Welby, and up to Aunt Thelma's room, which had Aunts Thelma and Pennina in it and, surprisingly, Sergeant Aloysius Mullins.

"—blew up in their faces," Mullins was saying, and stopped abruptly as Pam and Dorian came in. "Don't say I said it," he added, rather hurriedly. "Hello Mrs. North. Mrs. Weigand. Where's the Loot?"

Dorian said she did not know, and wished she did.

"The Loot had it right," Mullins said. "Somebody planted the stuff. Anyway, the D.A.'s afraid they did."

"Pam," Aunt Thelma said, "the most ridiculous thing has happened. Sometimes I can't believe she's my own sister."

Pam looked at Aunt Pennina.

"Lucinda," Aunt Thelma said. "She's—"

"Please, Aunt Thelma," Pam said. "Everything's getting so confused. What blew up, Sergeant?" Aunt Thelma looked at Pamela with severity. "Please, Aunt Thelma," Pam said. Mullins waited for things to subside. "Please, Sergeant Mullins," Pam said.

It was very simple. There were no fingerprints on the bottle one of the detectives working out of the District Attorney's office had found in Miss Thelma Whitsett's suitcase—none, at any rate, but his.

"The poor Joe," Mullins said, "should of used something."

And that, quite simply, made it blow up. There was, obviously, no reason why Miss Whitsett herself should have removed all fingerprints from a poison bottle and then have secreted it in her own suitcase—at least none anyone could think of, or would want to take to

court. There was every reason why anyone who had
put the bottle where it was found to incriminate Miss
Whitsett would have been careful not to leave his own
prints on it.

"He'd have to wipe it," Mullins pointed out. "Trust
to luck Miss Whitsett would touch it and leave prints.
Or that nobody would be bright enough to notice. Or
maybe he just didn't think about it at all." Mullins
paused. "You'd be surprised the guys who don't," he
added, out of long, if perhaps somewhat confusing,
experience.

"The inspector tried to argue maybe Miss Whitsett
did it that way to make it harder," Mullins told them.
"But this Thompkins wouldn't buy it and after he
thought it over, Arty—I mean the inspector, Mrs.
Weigand—wouldn't buy it himself. I gotta hand him
that. Also, everybody they talked to in Cleveland
pretty near died laughing." Mullins's own enjoyment,
although properly muted, was nevertheless apparent.
"So that lets you out of it, Mrs. North," he said.

It did, Pam thought. She no longer had an aunt to
protect.

"You don't need to look so pleased, Sergeant," Pam
told him. "You—"

"Pamela!" Aunt Thelma said, in that certain tone.
"Will you stop this nonsense and listen to me? Lucinda's gone."

"Gone?" Pam North repeated. "Gone where?"

"To the library," Aunt Pennina said. "I keep telling
Thelma—"

"Pennina!" Aunt Thelma said. "Show her the note.
I was just about to tell this man." She indicated
Mullins. An expression of foreboding crossed Mul-
lins's broad face. It was going to be screwy again.

It was, certainly. They looked at the note Aunt
Lucinda had left, confident that with it she made
everything entirely clear. They read: "Gone to the
library to find the place. Cripland not Gribland."

"Obviously," Aunt Pennina said, "she's lost her

place in some book or other and—" But then Aunt Pennina stopped and looked puzzled. "It really isn't very clear," she said.

Aunt Thelma should say not; she did.

"Gone to a place called Cripland or Gribland," she said. "What on earth?"

"Or where on earth," Pamela said. "I never heard of it. Did you, Dorian?"

Dorian had not. Mullins had not. Mullins got the policewoman, who was just preparing to leave. He learned that Miss Lucinda Whitsett had gone out during the morning, ostensibly to get stamps, but wearing a hat. "A pink hat," the policewoman said, and there was a kind of awe in her voice. "I had no instructions to detain her, Sergeant," she pointed out. "Merely to caution her."

It was then after three o'clock in the afternoon. Even without the note, it would have been apparent that Miss Lucinda had gone farther than the lobby, was in search of more than stamps. She had gone to a place named Cripland, *not* Gribland, which apparently could be found at the public library.

"Missing Persons," Sergeant Mullins said, and went for the telephone.

"Come on, Dorian," Pamela North said. "The library to start." She looked at the aunts. "You stay here," she told them. "Both of you. *Right* here."

"Pamela!" Aunt Thelma said, but the certain tone was wasted on a closing door.

The hills had grown taller as the little train chugged north. The trees were gold and red and green gold; the world burned gently, in beauty. The train had crept from Mount Kisco to Bedford Hills, shuddered and made Katonah. It had achieved Golden's Bridge and seemed intent on resting on its laurels, but then gone grumbling on to Purdys and to Croton Falls. Then it had gone around curves, up-grade, and a few miles ahead a white church steeple had appeared among the soft-burning trees. "Brewster next," a trainman said, hoarsely. "Brewster." The train puffed uphill beside a lake, hooted its triumph and slowly subsided at the Brewster station. It had still some miles to go before achieving Pawling, but Miss Lucinda had not. She went down steep steps onto a sunny platform, a slight woman in the middle sixties, holding firmly to a purse and a copy of the *Atlantic Monthly,* wearing a quite remarkable pink hat. Several people said, "Taxi, lady?" and from them she chose a jovial man who said "where-a you wanna go-a, please?" or something which sounded rather like it.

Miss Lucinda no longer had her memorandum, but she did not need it. Mr. Brisco, the taximan, knew the place. He said, however, "They're not home."

"They asked me to have a look at the place," Miss Lucinda said, firmly, and got into a very large car. There were two other passengers going in what Mr. Brisco chose to regard as Miss Lucinda's direction, but it took time to catch them. It was almost three o'clock when they left the station. But, started, Mr. Brisco drove very rapidly, keeping one hand on the wheel and waving to passing friends with the other. Even with one hand, Miss Lucinda decided after a few moments, he was very expert. It was not nervousness about his driving that made her wish he would go a little more slowly. She hoped she had been entirely clear in the note she had left for her sisters.

"—and a pink hat," Pam North said. "A *very* pink hat."

"Oh, of course," the young woman at the library information desk said. "I remember perfectly."

"Thank God for millinery," Dorian Weigand said. "Pam, I've got to see that hat."

"It's—" Pam began, starting to gesture a description. "It's no use, Dor." She turned back to the information girl, said, "It is the hat of my aunt. What did it—I mean, what did *she*—want?"

She had wanted to look at out-of-town telephone directories; specifically, at those which covered the area within a hundred miles or so of the city. Dorian and Pam, a good many hours later, followed Miss Lucinda's trail, knowing that the pink hat bobbed far ahead of them.

It was to be assumed that Miss Lucinda's interest in out-of-town telephone numbers was related to the death of Grace Logan; if it were not, if she were merely seeking to locate some suburban friend (named Cripland or Gribland?) the project was hopeless. Pam and Dorian had the obvious to go on, and went on it, wasting only a little time under the impression that Patterson, New York, was to be found in Westchester County; only a little more in finding that the Logan and Sandford country cottages, although presumably situated near Patterson, had Brewster telephone numbers. It was absurdly easy, then, since Miss Lucinda had made a pencil checkmark to identify the telephone listed under the name of Barton Sandford on Oak Hill Road. It was even easier, and more certain, when, on putting the book back in its stall, Pam dislodged from it Miss Lucinda's memorandum, made because Miss Lucinda always remembered anything once she had written it down.

But then it was a leap in the dark. It was hard to believe that little Miss Lucinda, alone, had gone adventuring into the country to find—to find what? Cripland? Gribland? But, with the time which had elapsed, it was inevitable to believe that she had gone somewhere.

It was Dorian, in the end, who was most sure. She could look at the aunts, not knowing them, with detachment. She could point out that, were Thelma Whitsett her sister, holding so tight a rein, she would herself go anywhere, on any adventure. But she could not guess why she had, as it appeared she had, taken off for the Sandford cabin.

"Not that there isn't reason to go there," she said. "To find out whether Mrs. Sandford is really there, or whether her typewriter is there. But how did your aunt get the idea? What does she know about it?"

The questions were unanswerable. So was the matter of Cripland or Gribland.

"All I'm sure of," Pam said, "is that it comes out of something she's read. You see, she is convinced that life repeats literature, just as she's sure everybody has a listed telephone number."

Perhaps, Dorian suggested, everybody did in Cleveland.

But Dorian stopped, then, because Pam was not listening. She was staring at the rank of telephone books, and her eyes were wide.

"Dor!" Pam said. "We were all wrong. Terribly wrong. We've got to go!"

She turned to go, and Dorian turned with her.

"Go where?" she asked.

"To Patterson or wherever it is," Pam said. "We've got to get there first. It's all upside down."

Mr. Brisco's concept of similarity in destination, as concerning passengers in his taxicab, had proved rather remarkably flexible. Knowing the area not at all, Miss Lucinda had at first no more than wondered vaguely about this. Perhaps, she had thought, it only seemed as if, after going five miles or so in one direction to deposit a man known as Jim—"be-a-seea-you-Jim"—Mr. Brisco had turned the car around in a narrow road and more or less driven the five miles back again. It had seemed to her, then, that it was stretching a point to think that Jim's destination had been on the way—"onaway"—to hers. It had mercly, she began to suspect, been in the same part of the country. She was not even sure about the county.

The second passenger was a young woman named Mizza Snyduh (which seemed improbable) and her destination was at least ten miles in what seemed to Miss Lucinda (but of course she *didn't* know the country) to be almost the opposite direction. This, then, was the way to Oak Hill Road; Jim had been merely a side issue. But do I, Miss Lucinda wondered, have to pay for all of this very considerable distance we are traveling? Mr. Brisco's taxicab did not have a meter; it was merely a car like any other car, although with a sign saying "Taxi" against the windshield, so there was no way of telling and she had not, before they started, thought to have any discussion of the fare. One didn't, in taxicabs; the meter told one. At least, it had been so in Cleveland. Miss Lucinda, riding rapidly if bewilderingly through a green and gold countryside, began to wonder if she had brought along enough money.

If she had—and if she had not, surely Mr. Brisco would understand, and probably take a check—there was, she began to feel, nothing immediate to worry about. Mr. Brisco was easy to trust, if not always to understand—he talked contentedly in his front seat, presumably to Mizza Snyduh, who did not, to be sure, answer, but perhaps to Miss Lucinda herself. The wind which swept into the open window on the driver's side presumably blew Mr. Brisco's words to pieces before they reached the rear seat. Certainly they arrived there in pieces. The countryside was beautiful and—this secretly felt, but best of all to feel—they were not reaching her destination with undue celerity. She was having time to think things out. This was one way of putting it. She was postponing an hour which might, which almost surely would, be evil. That was another way of putting it.

I have put my hand to the plow, Miss Lucinda told

herself, bobbing up and down as the big car hit uneven road, the pink hat a tossing banner. Darned be he who first cries hold enough. And of course when they get my note, someone will come to help; there will be someone to do the really difficult part. Miss Lucinda's mind winced away from the difficulty she expected. I wasn't foolish to come on alone, she told herself. Anyway, anyway—I can't always just sit and let Thelma—It is later than I think, Miss Lucinda thought. There is so little time. Dear Mr. Marquand; such a wonderful writer. It is my little fling.

The car turned off the main road into a much less considerable road, and from it into an even less considerable one—a dirt road, or almost. Surely, Miss Lucinda thought, this isn't Oak Hill Road. Surely Mr. Sandford doesn't—

"I bringa quick lika say," Mr. Brisco said, in triumph, and Miss Lucinda moved to get out. "Nota yet," he told her. "Thisa Mizza Snyduh. Youa next."

Miss Lucinda said, "Oh," and sat back. Mizza Snyduh got out and said, unexpectedly, "Goodbye now," having previously said nothing whatever. She paid Mr. Brisco and Miss Lucinda wondered how much, but felt it would be rude to try to see. Mr. Brisco backed the big car off the road, pulled it back on again, and started back the way they had come. "Notta far now lady," he said. "Pretty day."

They returned to the main road, turned back on it—Miss Lucinda was almost certain—the way they had come, and progressed gayly for several miles, Mr. Brisco happily waving at friends in passing cars. Then, without interrupting the salutation of the moment, or particularly slackening pace, he turned right abruptly into another secondary road, said, "Oaka Hill," and began resolutely to sound his horn. The reason was evident; most of the turns were blind and the road was narrow. Oh dear, Miss Lucinda thought. Oh dear me!

They went up a hill for what seemed another several

miles, turned off it into a patch of what was almost lawn, and stopped. Beyond the lawn there was a pleasant, small but sprawling house.

"Bringa quick," Mr. Brisco said, in pride of craftsmanship.

"This is it?" Miss Lucinda said.

"Thisa it," Mr. Brisco assured her. "You wanna wait?"

"Wait?" Miss Lucinda said. "Oh, no, I don't think you need wait. I'll—I'll telephone you when I want to leave."

Mr. Brisco looked back at her with apparent doubt. He looked with interest at her hat, which seemed to distract him, or perhaps to reassure him.

"Youadoc," he said. "Maybe she cutta off no?"

"No indeed," Miss Lucinda said politely. "How much is it, please?"

"Twoa doll," Mr. Brisco said. She paid him; she tipped him a quarter. She got out of the cab. It was not until the cab had backed, cut, backed once more and departed that it occurred to Miss Lucinda that Mr. Brisco might have meant to suggest that the telephone had been disconnected which would, certainly, make it difficult for her to telephone to be picked up. She had heard, she now remembered, that people sometimes had disconnected the utilities in country places which were closed up for the winter.

There was little now to suggest winter. The air here, fresher than it had been in the city, still was balmy and the breeze was gentle. It was true, of course, that the sun was already very low in the west; looking at her watch, Miss Lucinda was surprised to learn that it was only about four o'clock. She recalled to herself that the days were drawing in; that in another two hours or so it would be almost dark. She would want to start home before dark. Now—where should she begin? Inside, or out? She decided that inside would be most probable, if she was right at all. And oh, I hope I'm not, Miss Lucinda thought. But somebody has to make sure.

Getting inside a locked-up country cottage would have seemed, had she thought of it at all before this moment, a bridge to be crossed when she came to it, but now she had come to it unexpectedly and without plans. She went to the front door, as the most probable—and certainly most proper—place to start and, since it was not her house, she knocked. There was no response; she waited and knocked again, gently, since she was a gentle woman, but still with some decision—although not, as she thought to herself, loudly enough to wake the dead. Only after waiting again, did she try the door. It was, of course, locked. She had thought it would be.

She then, the pink hat bobbing, circled the house, trying first one window and then another. All the windows on the first side she tried were locked, and then she began to try those on the rear. They seemed to be locked too, and shades were drawn over them. All at once, Miss Lucinda began to feel forlorn. She had really been very foolish, now that she thought of it; no amount of understandable desire to help dear Thelma, or to escape momentarily from dear Thelma—and both things had, she realized, entered into it, together with whatever it was in her which had made her buy the pink hat—could exonerate her of having been foolish. Foolish, it now appeared, to no purpose. The back door was locked, as the front had been.

An electric meter was on the outside wall near the door and a little wheel was turning in it, as little wheels turn in electric meters. It was odd to be consoled by a little wheel, but Miss Lucinda momentarily was. Somehow, it seemed to bring the world closer. Miss Lucinda went on around the next corner and—the little wheel had been a token after all—found a window several inches open from the bottom. She tugged at it, and it opened fully.

Miss Lucinda looked around to be sure she was unobserved, because it would obviously be impossible to keep her skirt in its proper place while climbing in a window and, seeing no one who might observe her, did climb in the window. The pink hat was knocked a little crooked in the process, but not really damaged, and when she was standing—in a bedroom, as it turned out—Miss Lucinda straightened the hat. Then she began her search.

It was about the time Miss Lucinda, having broken and entered, straightened her pink hat and looked around a dim, apparently empty, bedroom that Pamela North took her car up the Twenty-third street ramp onto the West Side Highway and said, "Thank heaven!" Dorian Weigand, sitting a little shaken beside her, agreed in stronger terms.

"I know," Pam said, working into traffic on the elevated highway and picking up speed. "I *hate* trucks. Great, hulking things. Like the time Teeney was treed."

There was no answer to that but "What?" and Dorian made it.

"Like Great Danes," Pam said, "only it was really a police dog. They make Teeney furious and she always runs at them, only this one didn't run. I mean, not in the right direction. She was terribly frightened but she found a tree. I feel the same way about trucks."

"Once there I thought we were going to need a tree," Dorian said. "I thought you were going to settle for one of the pillars."

"He hadn't any business turning out," Pam said, turning out herself and going around, remarking, to her own steering wheel, that there ought to be a minimum just as much as a maximum. "Anyway, I had plenty of room, or almost."

Dorian had never seen a more alarmed face than that worn by a driver of a trailer truck who had observed, in West Street, Pamela North using what she now considered plenty of room. Of course, Dorian thought, I couldn't see my own. She shivered slightly.

"Whatever Jerry says," Pam North said, speeding up, "it's been fifteen thousand miles, anyway, since anything happened. And then he tried to pass on the right. So sixty or so more shouldn't be hard."

The last was clear enough. They were an estimated sixty miles from the place they guessed the Patterson cottages to be. At the moment, Pam seemed determined, if not destined, to make the distance in an hour.

"Who," Pam asked, honking angrily at a man she considered about to get in her way, "would have expected it of Aunt Lucinda? The reading one? And—how did she get onto it? It must have something to do with Cripland not Gribland. But I can't think what."

Neither could Dorian Weigand, holding onto the door handle, enjoying herself all the same. She hadn't, she thought, been this far into one of them since—oh yes, since she rode into New Jersey in the trunk of an elderly car, not by choice.* At least, this time, she was riding sitting up. She wished she had had time to leave a note for Bill, when she couldn't get him on the telephone. But he and Jerry would get together. They probably would come steaming after. Dear Bill!

"Jerry won't get in until after five," Pam said, as if Dorian had spoken. Trains of thought apparently had collided. Or perhaps, as Dorian had sometimes thought, Pam could jump without words. "They ought to get started by—oh, five thirty, unless Bill's lost somewhere. They'll have to take your car, of course."

They stopped at the Harlem toll bridge and paid their dime. They went on, jumping, up the Henry Hudson toward the Saw Mill.

"It will be dark before we get there, or almost," Pam said. "It'll be—I hope we get there first. I can't get over its being Aunt Lucy. It simply doesn't go with that hat."

_____
*Dorian's experience is recounted more fully in *Untidy Murder*. J. B. Lippincott Company. 1947.

"I don't know," Dorian said. "Perhaps it does, you know. Perhaps both things are a kind of breaking free."

Pamela North, taking the inner lane at sixty-five on the Saw Mill, chancing the parkway police, said with some fervor that she wished Aunt Lucy had been content to take it out in hats.

"After all," she said, "that hat is something you could do only once." She speeded up a little. "I hope this isn't too," she said, her voice very sober. "The poor little dear."

9

The bedroom in which Miss Lucinda first stood, instinctively straightening her hat, brushing at the skirt of her black silk dress with small, quick hands, was not a large room, and it was sparsely furnished. A bed, a chest, a chair—a lamp on the chest and another on a small table by the bed. The table teetered as one touched it, being unsteady on its legs. There were a few books on a shelf under the window by which Miss Lucinda had entered, and at some time the window had been left open during a rain, and the books were stained. A spread was thrown over a bare mattress on the bed and it did not lie evenly; almost without knowing what she did, Miss Lucinda brushed it into smoothness.

And the room was empty; not in it, surely, was what she expected, and feared, to find. She looked under the bed and found the floor dusty, but found nothing else. She went to the only door, opened it, and found herself in a living room unexpectedly large.

A stone fireplace held sway, unchallenged, over the wall opposite the door by which she entered. Ashes were piled high in the fireplace, almost covering the fire dogs; there was nothing to show whether it had been used the day before, or not since weeks before. There was a small window on either side of the fireplace, and to her right—toward the front of the house, next to the locked front door, there was a somewhat larger window. But the house was not faced toward the lowering sun of mid-October, and the room was dusky, filled with shadows.

There were many hiding places there, and this search took Miss Lucinda time. She sought at first without turning on the lights, seeking in the shadows. There were two sofas and several easy chairs, none of them new or newly covered, but all comfortable, inviting to relaxation. These things might, she thought, have been picked up second-hand some place, or moved from another house, or from a city apartment, when new furniture was bought to replace them. Under the windows on either side of the fireplace there were deep cupboards, and it was into them Miss Lucinda looked first—looked shivering a little as she opened each, relieved to find only the gear of summer life—tennis rackets, out-of-doors clothing for rainy days, a bridge table with its chairs, golf bags leaning in corners. Miss Lucinda, although in a certain way disappointed, was yet glad when she had done with the cupboards. She sought on.

She had looked behind each of the sofas, and under each, she had even looked up the chimney and been again at once disappointed and relieved to see, unobscured, the sky above, when she finally abandoned the living room. It would have been too obvious and, of course, in other ways impractical as a hiding place of what she was unhappily sure had been hidden. She went down the room toward the rear and through a door into a kitchen which, a little unexpectedly, contained such modern equipment as an electric range and refrigerator (its doors standing open), a sink (but with a single spout; cold water only, it was evident), a large deep freezing unit, and, less modernly, open shelves now holding little except a few cans. It was quite dark in the kitchen, and Miss Lucinda turned on the lights. The light showed her nothing, and here there was no occasion for a prolonged search. The kitchen, Miss Lucinda thought, did not lend itself to the concealment of what she sought. She left it, turning off the lights.

There were, occupying an el, two other rooms on the ground floor—a much larger, now sun-flooded, bedroom and a reasonably modern bath opening off it. The bedroom had been, Miss Lucinda decided, built onto the original house in fairly recent years; its windows were larger, its whole feeling more of present times. It held twin beds, two chests with mirrors and a dressing table with another; there were two easy chairs, and french doors opened to a terrace. Connected with the room there was what Miss Lucinda— now more hesitant than ever, but forcing herself on— found to be a rather large closet.

The closet was filled with a woman's clothes, and this time not only with garments for summer's warm, lazy days. There were several dresses obviously meant for town wear; two coats in addition to a light coat for summer evenings, and several hats—the latter nondescript, Miss Lucinda thought, restraightening her own. To search thoroughly in the closet, Miss Lucinda had to move into it, among the hanging garments, parting them. They were faintly, pleasantly, fragrant.

And, Miss Lucinda thought, coming out of the closet without having found what she sought, there was now no real doubt she was right—no doubt at all. It was as if a little light had gone out somewhere, because Miss Lucinda had hoped—had *so* hoped— that she would be proved wrong after all. (Of course, Miss Lucinda thought in an aside, there might be a lot of other clothes; a really large wardrobe. In which case—)

There was, Miss Lucinda decided, no use seeking such escapes from logic. She must, as the English said—what charming books the English women wrote, to be sure. Dear Sheila Kaye-Smith—face *up* to it. She must, in her small way, prove master of her soul, as

Mr. Henley had so famously been. She must not, as something prompted—but not her soul, certainly—pick up the telephone there on the table between the twin beds and ask for the return of Mr. Brisco. She must not—nevertheless, it might be as well to find out whether, if she wished, she could. She picked up the telephone and listened. There was only the faintest of empty sounds. She jiggled, but there was not even a clicking in her ears. Presumably the telephone had been disconnected for the winter. Mr. Brisco had been right. She was not, it appeared, entirely the captain of her fate; the New York Telephone Company also was involved. However—

However, Miss Lucinda told herself, sitting down in one of the chairs and smoothing black silk over her knees, first things must come first. Second might come how she got back to—to any place. The first thing was, where was it?

Not, apparently, in the house itself and, now, Miss Lucinda realized she had been doing the easiest thing first. It would be outside somewhere, under ground—she shivered again; surely it was really getting cooler as the sun sank—or in—why, of course! In the cellar. That was the most likely place of all. The question remained, however, was there a cellar? She had not noticed any door which seemed likely to lead to one.

She got up from the chair and noticed that the room was now by no means as sunny as it had been. It was, she thought, getting late very early. On this point, her watch confirmed her; it was now long after five. There was not much daylight left. Miss Lucinda went more briskly through the rooms, looking for a cellar. In the kitchen—she had, she realized now, dismissed the kitchen rather cavalierly on her first time round—she found an inconspicuous door and, opening it, the unquestionable smell of a cellar. Air which was almost cold, and certainly was damp, came up from it. Miss Lucinda shivered again and tightened about her the short, inadequate coat which had, early in the day, seemed only a nuisance. She peered downward into the dark. She sought, and did not find, a light switch.

In country cottages, she decided, there must be flashlights, and the most likely place for them would be—she began pulling out the few kitchen drawers available. She found two flashlights in the second drawer, but the first of them apparently was broken. At least, when Miss Lucinda pressed the button, nothing happened. The second produced a tired, yellow radiance. She hoped it would be enough. She returned to the cellar door, opened it—it apparently closed by itself, as a result of something in its hinges—and let yellow light trickle down steep stairs. It looked to Miss Lucinda like a place for rats.

My head is bloody but unbowed, Miss Lucinda told herself and went cautiously down the steep stairs. The door closed behind her.

"I don't," Pam North said, coming to what certainly was almost a full stop at the entrance to the Hawthorne circle, "see how she got onto it. I thought all along it was the other way around, of course. And she just pulls it out—out of that pink hat." Pam swung around the circle into the Taconic State parkway. "It'll be dark before we get there," she said.

The speed limits on the Taconic State are slightly more lenient than on the Saw Mill, where only forty is allowed. On the Taconic, one may legally do forty-five. Pam, encouraged, reached toward seventy. "While it's still light," she said.

"You don't," Dorian told Pamela, "actually know she *is* onto it. I mean, you don't know she has it right. As a matter of fact, Pam, you don't know you have it either."

She was invited to tell any other way it could have been. She hesitated.

"Anyway," Pam said, "we'll know in an hour or so, probably. If we"—she pulled around a car doing a mere sixty; she told her steering wheel that some people oughtn't to be allowed on parkways, which were for people going somewhere—"don't get lost," she said. "Unless—Dor, whatever made her? The frail, sweet, little—Dor, it scares me!"

"At the moment," Dorian said, "we scare me too. Particularly if you're right. I hope Bill—"

What he had, Inspector O'Malley told Weigand, was nothing but a hunch. Suppose he was right, where was he?

"So you've got a theory about this Mrs. Sandford," he said. "You think maybe you know where she is. So—what have you got? Where does the Logan kill come in?"

Bill could, he said, only guess. He would guess that, somehow, Mrs. Logan had found out about Mrs. Sandford and, because of that, had been fed cyanide.

"It's screwy," the inspector said. He sat behind his desk, red of face. "That Thompkins," he said. "Like you, Bill. Making it hard." He grew redder. "And," he said, "she's the aunt of this Mrs. North of yours. Don't forget that. What've you got to say about that?"

Bill knew how the inspector felt. He said so.

"You want to make captain, don't you?" the inspector asked. "Do you or don't you?"

"Right," Bill said. "Sure I do."

"Well?" the inspector demanded.

Conversations with Arty often got out of hand, Bill Weigand thought sadly. If the Norths were anywhere involved, and it seemed they frequently were, the inspector could no more avoid buzzing angrily, like an incensed bumblebee, around that fact than he could—Bill's mind paused. "Jump through the moon." The phrase came to him unsolicited, unwanted, and for a moment unrecognized. Oh—it was Pam who said that, presumably feeling that jumping through the moon was a feat even more unlikely than jumping over it.

"Well?" Inspector O'Malley repeated.

"Look," Bill Weigand said. "You know as well as I do, sir—better than I do—that Thompkins can't take it to court. Not with the fingerprint angle. Not with the reports from Cleveland. We'll just have to give that one up."

The "we" was generous, Bill thought. Arty would have to give it up. And Arty would, Arty already had. Much as he might like to see any aunt of Mrs. Gerald North's in as much hot water as was available, Inspector Artemus O'Malley was a cop, and knew the score. He could still fume about it, but he'd lost his candy.

"You want to have another go at Sandford, then?" Inspector O'Malley said, tacitly admitting he had given up the candy. "But there's this other angle?"

That was the size of it, Bill said. He had as good as been warned off. But that was when he was unofficial, or as unofficial as a cop who is never off duty can well get.

"Who do they think they are?" Inspector O'Malley asked the world. "This is our town, ain't it?"

"Right," Bill said. "Our town. Our murder."

"What you do," O'Malley said, "is get hold of this Sandford. Make him come clean about his wife. That's what you do. Who do those guys think they are?"

"You'll clear it with them if there's a squawk?" Bill asked.

He was damned right the inspector would. Who did they think they were?

It was unnecessary to tell the inspector that they thought, rightly, that they were agents of the Federal Bureau of Investigation; that they thought they had something coming along they didn't want tampered with; that they suspected the local police might upset their much prized apple-cart.

"The way I look at it," Inspector O'Malley told Lieutenant Weigand. "Murder comes first. I don't give a damn who this Sandford is. You put it up to him."

Bill Weigand said, "Right." He went.

He went, he drove to Barton Sandford's apartment; he did not find Barton Sandford. He drove uptown to Gimo's Restaurant in the East Fifties. Sandford was

not there. From Gimo's, he telephoned his apartment.
Nobody answered his call. It was after five, then;
Dorian and Pam were having quite an afternoon for
themselves. He tried the North apartment, and again
got no answer. It was only then he realized how surely
he had expected Dorian and Pam to be at the Norths',
their day's work—whatever it had been—done; the
time for cocktails arrived. It was only then he realized
he was beginning to be worried.

There are few greater fallacies than the belief that,
because a man can write well enough to get books
published, he can make a speech to several hundred
women without falling flat on his face. This fact Jerry
considered morosely in the club car as he sipped, also
morosely, at the Pennsylvania Railroad's version of a
martini.

"I was terrible," the shaggy man in the next seat
told Jerry North. "Don't tell me I stank." He drank
scotch.

"You were all right," Jerry told Ferguson, with
gloomy insincerity. "How about another drink?"

"I might as well," Ferguson said. "Or shoot myself.
You talked me into it, remember."

"You were fine," Jerry said. "As good as anybody."

"God!" Ferguson said, simply.

Jerry hoped that Pam hadn't got herself into trouble.
He hoped she had stayed home, or gone to the Welby
and held the hands of aunts. He hoped he never had to
hear writers speak again. He hoped he never again had
to scratch at a hotel's luncheon version of broiled
spring chicken. He had little confidence in the fulfill-
ment of any of these hopes.

"Tell you what," Ferguson said, from the middle of
his new scotch. "I write 'em, you sell 'em. How's
that?"

"Next time," Jerry told him. "You've got Boston
coming up Friday, remember. Can't get out of that
now. Very fine audience at Boston."

"God," Ferguson said, and finished the scotch. He looked out the window. "Newark," he said, in the same tone. "You going along to Boston?"

"Kennely'll be along on that one," Jerry told him. Which is something, he told himself.

"God," said Ferguson. "I should have been a painter."

"They have to show up at shows," Jerry told him, and finished the martini.

"A traveling salesman," Ferguson said. He qualified it.

Now, Jerry thought, we get the Hemingway routine.

"Speaking of Hemingway," Ferguson said, unexpectedly, "what the hell was the idea—"

Hemingway lasted them through the tunnel. It lasted Ferguson into a taxicab and Jerry into another. Whatever else you could say, Hemingway was durable. Perhaps it would have been better if Ferguson had talked about Hemingway at the luncheon.

Jerry's cab struggled in traffic, taking many minutes to get nowhere; half an hour to get where it was going. It was some time after five then. But Jerry need not have hurried. The apartment was empty, even of Martha. It took him several minutes of anxious search to find Pam's note which, for reasons not immediately apparent to her husband, she had tucked under one of the telephones. Jerry used the telephone.

There she was now, Bill Weigand thought, hearing the telephone ringing through the apartment door. And here he was, on the wrong side of the door, digging anxiously for his keys, convinced that each summons from the telephone would be its last. He jammed key into keyhole, pushed resentfully at the door, reached the telephone and said, "Yes."

"Bill," Jerry said. "Pam left a note. Dorian's with her."

Bill sat down. It seemed like a good idea.

"Go ahead," he told Jerry North. Jerry went ahead.

"Here's the note," he said. "Listen. 'It's Aunt Lucy

now, and I was all wrong the whole time. We've gone to Patterson.' She signed it and then added a post-script. 'Don't worry, Dorian's with me.' Patterson?"

"Damn," Bill said.

"I know," Jerry said. "Feel the same way. What's Patterson New Jersey got to do with it?"

"New York," Bill said. "At least, I suppose so. The Logans have a summer place up there. The Sandfords too. Damn it to hell."

"What about Aunt Lucy?" Jerry said. "I've been in Philadelphia all day."

"I don't know," Bill said. "I'll find out. You're home?"

Jerry was. He would wait.

It did not take long. Bill called Jerry North back with the information, imparted it crisply.

"Pam's taken our car," Jerry said. "We'll have to use yours. Want me to—"

"I'll pick you up," Bill told him. "It's—I'm afraid they've really stuck their necks out this time."

"When I get *hold* of her," Jerry promised him. "I'll be downstairs," he added.

The cellar was very small, extending only under part of the kitchen, and under none of the rest of the house. Once, Miss Lucinda decided, it had been used as a root cellar. Now it had in it what was apparently a heater of some sort, a few bare shelves and, obscurely, an ancient rocking chair. It was damp and smelled of mold, and the dripping yellow light from her torch did hardly more than intensify, by dimly contrasting with, utter darkness. But Miss Lucinda could discover that the floor was cemented, and she went very slowly, very carefully, very resolutely over the floor, all the time hearing sounds which might be made by rats. Once, in a corner, her light picked up a reflection and she thought it came from the eyes of some animal, from a rat's eyes, and almost screamed before she realized that rats, unpleasant as they are in all particulars, are commonly not cyclopean and discovered that the reflection came from a tiny shard of broken glass.

But she did not find what she expected—indication that the cement floor had been broken and then replaced. She could not be sure of this; it was not a subject on which she was at all informed. But she was certain there would be something to show—an irregularity, a difference in color—something to be seen if one looked for it. And, however she looked for it, there was nothing.

Then it must be outside, and that was—well, clearly, that was beyond her. That was a labor of Hercules, or at least of several men with—with shovels. (Or was it spades?) It was, Miss Lucinda reflected, Adam who delved, while Eve span. She would have to get back to somebody and—well, spin her yarn. She could, she assured herself, a tale unfold. It was absurd, indeed, that no one else, apparently, had noticed how all this and the famous one ran parallel, or almost. And then she thought—goodness, whatever did I say in that note? She remembered very well, however; and remembered she had still been wrong. But would anyone, then, be able to make anything of it? Make something of it and—come?

Miss Lucinda started for the steep staircase. She must, in some way, get back.

Then she heard, above, the unmistakable sound of people walking, and hurried toward the staircase. They had come after all. They— She heard voices and, half way up the steep stairs, stopped. They were not the voices of anyone who would, having got her note and understood it, have come after her.

"—if she is, it is," a man's voice said. "We know that. And she is—"

The voice was familiar to Miss Lucinda, near the top of the cellar stairs now, listening close to the door. It was—why, it was Paul Logan's voice! What was he doing here?

"—only guessing," a girl's voice said, and this voice

Miss Lucinda did not recognize. But if it was a girl it was probably Rose Hickey's daughter. What was her name? Lynn—that was it.

The two were moving around as they talked. They were opening things and closing them. It sounded as if they were looking for something, as she had been. She could tell them it would be no use. But why were they here?

"—talked yourself into it," the girl said. "Trying to prove to Mrs. North and that friend of hers that you and—"

They went, moving with the light, quick steps of youth, into the large bedroom, and Miss Lucinda could no longer hear what they said. Very cautiously, she opened the door. Now she could hear, or almost hear.

"—typewriter, for one thing—" Paul Logan said, and then must, from the muffled sound, have put his head into the closet or, possibly, under a bed. The girl said nothing, but appeared to be opening and closing the drawers of the chests. That puzzled Miss Lucinda. *It* couldn't be in one of those.

"—with her," Paul said, taking his head, apparently, out of whatever it had been in. "That would be the payoff. If you don't think the clothes are."

"I'll admit the clothes," the girl said. "How do you figure the kitchen?"

Paul Logan said something which Miss Lucinda could not hear. She could hear the girl say, "Well," doubtfully, as if in reply.

They had finished with the big bedroom and were coming out of it. Miss Lucinda gently closed the cellar door and waited. They went into the living room. She opened the door again, but could only hear them moving about; hear the sound of voices, but not the words. Then, unexpectedly, Paul Logan raised his voice.

"—won't hold them a minute," he said. "Probably a bluff from the start. So where do they come back?"

The girl said something Miss Lucinda could not hear.

"You're damned right," Paul said. "That's where they come back. Particularly since your mother—"

The voice faded out again. It faded back in.

"I know she couldn't," Paul said. "I realize that, Lynn. Eventually, they'd get it out of her."

Lynn said something.

"That isn't good enough," Paul said. "You have to get away with it. I'm not going to let—"

But what he was not going to let did not appear. His voice was muffled again to Miss Lucinda, listening at her door, trying to piece it together. She could not make it come out. Paul Logan and Lynn Hickey were looking for something. But if she was right, they were not looking for the right thing. But, if not that, what? And what were the missing words which would fill in the crossword puzzle of their speech?

None of it, and this was clear, fitted in with what she was certain was the truth. When people talked of "getting away with something" it was—well, it was a very strange way to talk; a frightening way to talk. Of course, nowadays people often talked strangely; perhaps they talked of "getting away with" quite innocent things. It must be that, in this case; they must be there, although looking in chest drawers did not indicate it, on the same unpleasant errand as herself. If so—

Miss Lucinda opened her door further. Paul was always such a sweet boy, although certainly under his mother's thumb. (Although now he sounded resolute enough.) No doubt Lynn was a sweet girl, really. If what they were saying—had been saying, since now she could hear nothing—made her obscurely uneasy, it was obviously because there was so much which she had not heard. Snatches of conversation could be so misleading. She had read a short story recently in which everything turned on that, although in the end it was all cleared up. It was ridiculous for her to be uneasy; for her, since they must have the same purpose as she had—and since they unquestionably had means of transportation, which she did not have—not to join them. Before they finished and—

Miss Lucinda realized that she no longer heard any sound in the house, no sound of movement or of voices. Oh, she thought, I've waited too long. I've just *stood* here and let them go without me. I—

She opened the door and hurried out into the kitchen. She knew then, immediately, that she had been too late. The house was, except for herself, empty again. They had given up their search; since there were two of them they had been much quicker; they might have been in the house for some time before she heard them.

It was quite dark now in the house. Even the faint yellow seepage of light from the almost exhausted flashlight in Miss Lucinda's hand was visible in the shadowy kitchen.

It did not help her much in the even more shadowy living room, and her progress across it, although she tried to hurry, was slow. But she reached the front door, and opened it after only a brief struggle with the knob of the snap lock, and stepped out into the open. It was not really dark yet; not entirely dark. It was the gloaming—lovely word.

She did not see anybody, or any car, although she had certainly expected a car. It was as if Paul Logan and Lynn had stepped out of the house and vanished in the dusk. It was as if—

Miss Lucinda did not know which way to go to find them, but she nevertheless stepped away from the house, walked a little way across the lawn in front of it.

She did not hear any sound. She felt only a great, stunning pain in her head. Then it was all dark.

10

At a quarter after six, Pam and Dorian passed the pedestaled elephant in Somers; at six thirty their car hesitated at the fork just outside Brewster on Route 22. Patterson was ahead, Brewster itself to the left. Oak Hill Road was, presumably, in the vicinity of Patterson. Pam swung the car left.

They would, clearly, never find Oak Hill Road unaided, and Brewster was the place to find aid. There would be somebody there who knew.

"A taxi driver," Dorian said. "Country taxi drivers know everything."

There was a short, heavy, beaming man when they parked in front of the Brewster railroad station. He was sitting in a car marked "Taxi" and Pam went up to him. She said she wanted to find Oak Hill Road in Patterson.

"Sure-a," said Mr. Brisco. "Looka. You go uppa Twenta maybe foura fivea mile, thena left and *thena* right maybe eighta nina mile thena uppa hill and atta top—"

"Please," Pam said. "I'm afraid I—"

"There you be-a careful," Mr. Brisco said. "You goa thisa way—no place. You comma right back. You goa the righta way, Oaka Hill maybe threea foura

170

miles." He beamed. "Easy," he said. "Just like-a I say."

"The Sandford cottage," Pam said. "You know-a—I mean, you know where it is?"

"Sure," Mr. Brisco said. "I taka lady there. Alla closed up."

Pamela North knew relief.

"And brought her back, then?" she said. "A lady with a pink hat?"

"That-a-hat!" Mr. Brisco said. "Beaut. Pritt. My daught she like-a hat like that. Middle daughter. Sucha hat!"

"Yes," Pam said. "It's—it's quite a hat. Did you bring the lady back?"

"Bringa back?" Mr. Brisco said. "Why bringa back?"

"You mean she stayed there?"

"Sure," Mr. Brisco said. "Why-a not?"

There were, Pam thought, a good many answers to that, but none relevant.

"Can you guide us there?" she said. "For whatever it would be, of course?"

"Twoa doll," Mr. Brisco said. "You ready now?"

Pam was, as soon as she was back in the car.

"You like-a goa fast?" Brisco asked, as she departed. She did indeed. She said so. She backed and turned and Mr. Brisco's car leaped out of its stall and dashed down Main Street. Mr. Brisco's hand waved gayly out of his window and at first Pam thought he was signaling her. But then she saw that people on the sidewalk waved back.

Mr. Brisco's car reached the intersection of Route 22 and stopped for a light. It started up again, going left. It went very rapidly; it was first a car in the beam of Pam's headlights; then it was two red lights, retreating. Pam pressed down hard. When Mr. Brisco saida fast he meanta fast.

The way was as tortuous as it had sounded and,

after the first clean run of some miles, the pace slackened. Mr. Brisco went left, slowing, holding his hand out in signal, and the road became more winding. He turned and turned again, and Pam hung on grimly.

"What a place to live!" Dorian said, with feeling, holding on. They bumped.

"Probably a short-a cut," Pam said. "I wish—"

But Mr. Brisco had disappeared over a hill and around a curve. She abandoned speech to spurt after him. He was rounding another curve. She hoped that, when he next turned off, he would wait for her to catch up. His lights, and Pam's behind him, tore at the darkness.

"I don't," said Pamela North, fighting a heavy car which tried to ride doubtful shoulders, "see why we don't always have daylight saving. Doubled. Who wants it light in the morning?"

"Cows, from all I've heard," Dorian said. "Whew!"

"Like them," Pam said. "I—"

She suddenly braked furiously, and the tires whined on the pavement. Mr. Brisco slowed down as rapidly as he took off. Now he motioned her alongside.

His car stood just short of a narrow road, inadequately paved.

"Oaka Hill," he said. "Mist Sandford firsta house."

He did not himself, Pam gathered, plan to continue farther.

"Two-a cars," he explained. "Notta much-a space."

Dorian, nearest, gave him two dollars; added half a dollar for good measure and his engaging personality. He waved as they started, turning up the narrow road. Behind them, he turned into the road, backed out again. He was gone. The countryside felt the emptier.

The narrow road twisted—climbed and twisted. Now the powerful lights were on it, now they glared at trees on one side and now at bushes on the other. Pam drove at thirty, then at twenty, shifted to second. They were bright and noisy in the night, announcing their coming to whoever, whatever, might listen. An animal stood for a second in their path, facing the lights—a big animal. With a bound it was gone, a white tail flickering for an instant in the lights.

"I'd hate to run over a deer," Pam said. "Do you suppose we've passed it?"

It was hard to tell; in the end they almost did, but Dorian, forcing her vision into the darkness, saw faint markings to the right and the little lawn beyond them. Pam stopped, backed a few feet carefully, and turned in. As she turned, her lights flooded the front of a low, sprawling house. The house was lighted and after a moment, the door opened and a man was standing in it. Pam cut her motor, and dropped the beam of her lights.

The man was Barton Sandford. He said, "Who is it?" in a loud voice. He said, "Who're you looking for?"

"Mrs. North," Pam said. "For—" She paused.

"Oh," Sandford said. "Well—come on in."

Pam and Dorian went on. It was unexpectedly chilly out of the car; unexpectedly quiet with the motor stilled. They went into the house and Sandford closed the door after them.

"Well," he said, "this is unexpected. Fine, though."

"We're looking for my aunt," Pam said.

"Your aunt?" Sandford said. "What the hell? I mean—" He smiled doubtfully; the smile crinkled the corners of his wide-spaced eyes. "How would one of your aunts get up here?" he asked. "The—the one the police thought might have—?" He broke off, politely.

"The littlest one," Pam said. "The one with the pink hat. Aunt Lucinda."

"Pink hat?" Barton Sandford repeated.

"I don't think you met her," Pam said. "For—for some reason, she decided to come here. I don't know why. We were worried about her, of course."

"Hell yes," Sandford said. "I'd think so. Can't see why she'd come here. Unless—" He paused. "Anyway, she didn't," he said. "Or, if she did, she's gone now. I've had time to—" He stopped again. "It's all a hell of a note," he said, and his voice sounded troubled. "Come on, I'll build up a fire."

He led them into the living room; took paper and kindling and logs from a cupboard; talked as he laid the fire.

"Got here about ten minutes ago," he said. "I've—I've looked the place over pretty thoroughly. For—" He became very busy for a moment. Then he spoke without turning. "For Sally," he said. "I—I'm afraid she's been living here. Not traveling around as she said. Living right here for—I don't know what for." He struck a match and the paper flared. He stood up and turned to face them. His voice now was very troubled.

"I got afraid," he said. "Of—well, you can guess what. Came up hoping I could prove she hadn't been here. But—" He stood silent for a moment and shook his head. "The typewriter's here," he said. "Her typewriter. The one she's been writing the letters on—to her aunt, now and then to me. It's right here. I'm afraid it has been all along. And if that's true—Sally has."

"But she's not now?" Pam said. "You say you've looked?"

He'd looked, he said. Not that there was much need to. The house had been dark when he came; he had lighted lights. It had felt empty. "You know," he said. "You can tell." Nevertheless, he had called Sally's name and looked into each of the rooms. She was not there. But—her clothes were. The clothes he supposed she had taken with her on her trip; the clothes she must have taken with her.

"She could have been away and come back," Pam said. "It could have been that way."

He shook his head again. He said he wished it could. He said, "Come on, I'll show you."

He led them down the long room for a few steps, to a

table with a chair by it—and a portable typewriter,
open, on it. There was a sheet of unheaded paper in
the typewriter; on it had been typed:

Denver, Thursday, 10–19

Dear Bart:

I think I've got it about worked out. Anyway, I'll
come back and you and I can

"You see," Barton Sandford said, "something interrupted her. This afternoon—this evening? Perhaps it
was your aunt, Mrs. North. But—you can see what
she planned. You see how she dated it?"

"Day after tomorrow," Pam said. "So that—"

"So that she could take a plane and fly to Denver
and mail it," Sandford said. "Then, I suppose, fly back
here. I suppose she'd drive over to—oh, say Danbury,
where she wasn't known, park the car some place, go
into New York and fly to whatever city she—she
thought was a good place, and mail a letter. I suppose
sometimes go to one city and mail the letter and to
another and pick up some hotel stationery for—for the
next time."

"Why didn't she merely take the typewriter along
with her?" Dorian asked. "I mean, she apparently
hasn't any stationery from a Denver hotel, and has to
use plain paper. If she took the typewriter along—"

But Sandford was shaking his head. He said he'd
show her. He reached under the table and brought out
the cover of the portable. He fitted it on. "Now," he
said to Dorian, "take hold of it, Miss Hunt." Dorian
did; she lifted. The cover came off. "Try to lock it,"
Sandford said. Dorian tried. She lifted again. The
cover came off.

It had, Sandford said, been broken for months, so
that it could not be carried by its handle. Presumably
it could be strapped together, tied together, in some

fashion but—he shrugged. They had never tried that; they had got out of the habit of considering the typewriter as in any real sense a portable one. Probably tying it together somehow would never have occurred to Sally, nor, had he been in her place, to him.

"But—" Dorian began, her voice puzzled.

Pam interrupted; she interrupted quickly.

"If Aunt Lucy came here and found—well, your wife, Mr. Sandford. Then—*where is my aunt, Mr. Sandford?*"

"Not here," Sandford said. "I'm—"

"You didn't look everywhere," Pam told him. "You—you just called for your wife and looked in rooms quickly. I—*Aunt Lucy!*" Pam's clear voice rose high. *"Aunt Lucy?"*

"It's no good, Mrs. North," Sandford said. "I'm— I'm damned afraid—" He shook his head slowly; he seemed puzzled, uneasy, as if he were trying to press down some fear rising in his own mind. "But Sally wouldn't—"

"You're afraid, Mr. Sandford," Pam North said. "You know you are! We've got to—"

The lights of a car flooded into the room, moved across it as the car turned. Sandford started; then stood motionless for a moment; then moved toward the door. He said *"Now* what?" and pulled the door open. The lights of the car went out. A voice said, "Bart? You here?"

"What the—" Barton Sandford said. "Oh. Paul?"

"What's going on here?" Paul Logan asked from the darkness. Then he was at the door, his arm around the shoulders of Lynn Hickey. "What's up? We saw the lights and—" He broke off, looking at Pamela North and Dorian. "Oh," he said. "You got here."

"We're looking for my aunt," Pam said. "And—and Mrs. Sandford. What're you—?"

"Picking up some things from our place," Paul Logan said, quickly. "Starting back and saw the lights. Figured—well, we'd better look into it. Didn't know it was you, Bart. Figured it might be—"

It was his turn to break off, although he was not interrupted. He looked across the room, his gaze fixed.

He said, *"Lynn, it's here!"* He looked around at the others. "Here now," he said. "It wasn't."

The three of them looked at him. Sandford spoke first; spoke slowly. He said he didn't get it.

"Wasn't when?" he said. "What're you talking about, Paul?"

"The typewriter," Lynn said. "Tell him, Paul."

"We were here—oh, an hour or so ago," Paul said. "I knew where the key was, you know. We—" He hesitated. "We came to look for the typewriter," he said. "Or—or some trace that Sally was living here. Wasn't where she said she was. Because—" He looked at Pam North. "You know why," he said.

"I know," Pam said. "Then?" She looked at Barton Sandford. He spoke quickly.

"Then—*she's been here since,"* he said. "Had the typewriter hidden so you didn't find it, Paul. Got it out. Started one of the letters then—then she must have been interrupted."

"My aunt," Pam said. "You—she wasn't here, Mr. Logan? A—a little woman with a—a strange pink hat." She paused. "A funny hat," she said. "Meant—meant to be gay." The clear voice trembled a little.

"There wasn't anybody here," Paul said. "And— the typewriter wasn't here."

"It must have been," Sandford said. "You just didn't find it. Maybe—maybe she put it down in the cellar. Did you look there?"

Paul Logan looked puzzled. Then he said, "Oh, damn. I forgot."

"The point is," Dorian said, "she must have been here within—within an hour? Between the time you left, Mr. Logan, and the time Mr. Sandford came.

About ten minutes before we did?" The last was a question, to Sandford.

"Just about," he said. "I put the car—a hired car, since she's got ours—in the shed and then came on in. About ten minutes."

"The other car," Dorian said. "Your own car. Was it in the shed, or wherever you usually put it?"

"No," Sandford said. "It wasn't there. She must have taken it when she left. When she left this time." He hesitated. He spoke slowly. "If your aunt surprised her, Mrs. North," he said, "Sally might have taken—made her go along. Or—" He stopped abruptly.

"Or killed her?" Pam said. "Is that what you mean, Mr. Sandford. Or killed her? Because—because you're saying, now, your wife killed Mrs. Logan, aren't you?"

"No," Sandford said. "I don't give a damn what it looks like. No!"

"Because if you're saying that—" Pam said, and stopped, listening.

Somewhere there was a faint, miserable sound; a sound like a whimper. It seemed to come from a long way off, yet it was in the house. They turned, locating the source; trying to locate the source.

"The bedroom!" Paul Logan said, and was the first to move. Pam North was behind him and then the others.

The bedroom was empty, but the sound was there—the little whimpering sound. It was easy to trace, now. Paul turned quickly, reached for the closet door. In an instant a tiny, ageing woman was in his arms; a woman in a dusty black silk dress and a short, light coat; a woman bare-headed and with blood on her gray-blond hair.

"Cold, so cold," Aunt Lucinda Whitsett said, her eyes closed, the words uncertain on her lips, slurring a little. "Won't understand about Cripun. Won't—"

Paul had carried her into the center of the room; was

carrying her into the living room and to the fire. They were almost there when Aunt Lucinda opened her eyes. She looked up at Paul Logan.

"You tried to kill me," she said. "Hit me and wanted to kill me. Why, Paul?"

Paul Logan stared down at the little woman in his arms—arms apparently so much stronger than anyone would have thought.

"I—" he said.

But she had closed her eyes again; seemed again to have drifted away from them. She raised one hand to her head.

"Hurts so," she said and then, "I had a hat. A pret—" The voice faded out.

Traffic had been thinner when Weigand, with Jerry North beside him and Mullins in the seat behind, had gone along West Street. They could not use the siren, for several months silenced in tribute to national panic, but the red police lights helped. For the Buick there was no speed limit on the West Side Highway, nor on the parkways beyond; once in Westchester, the siren could sound again, but there it was not often called for. So they had gone considerably faster than Pam and Dorian had gone before them. They passed Brewster at seven fifteen, the siren wailing at a red traffic light, causing a Cadillac on collision course to pause so abruptly that its front end drooped, ridiculously bowing.

"You'll have to take it slower now, Loot," Mullins said, from the back seat. "I was here in the daytime. I can find it, but we'll have to take it easy."

"Right," Bill Weigand said. "You'd better, friend."

"O.K., Loot," Mullins said. "I told you it was a screwy one."

"How long?" Jerry demanded.

"Fifteen minutes," Mullins said. "Maybe twenty. It's quite a ways out."

"They'll be all right, Jerry," Bill said, but the speed crept up again.

"What makes you think so?" Jerry asked. "What the hell makes you think so?"

"I can't tell," Pam said, hopelessly. She was on her knees beside Miss Lucinda, who was in a low chair by the fire. "Damn nurse's aiding. All I remember is how to make a sling. You see, Dor."

Dorian put fingers on the tiny wrist. She said, "Her pulse seems steady enough." She felt again for a moment. "Strong enough," she said.

Miss Lucinda moaned. Faintly, she said she was cold. Then, in a stronger voice, she said, "I feel all wet."

She was fairly wet, at least about the head. They had tried to wash the blood from her hair; had held cold cloths to her forehead. The wound did not look deep, but how could a layman tell?

"Miss Whitsett," Paul Logan said, and bent close to her. "What did you mean, I hit you? What did you mean?"

"Leave her alone," Pam said.

"Now, Pamela, don't be so fussy," Miss Lucinda said, in an unexpectedly firm voice. "I know what I know. You're like Thelma."

"Thank heaven you're all right," Pam said. "But you must be quiet, Aunt Lucy."

"Like Thelma," Aunt Lucinda repeated, with even more firmness. "Always telling me to be quiet. What I mean is, young man, you hit me. On the head. Carried me back into that closet. I suppose you thought I was dead. But I wasn't." She paused. "Unless it was you," she said, and looked at Lynn Hickey, standing behind Paul.

"It wasn't either of us, Miss Whitsett," Lynn Hickey said. The crispness was out of her voice, now. Logan, standing again, put an arm around her shoulders, and she seemed glad of the arm. "Really it wasn't," she said.

"Sneaking around," Miss Lucinda said. "You can't deny it. And when I went after you, because the telephone wasn't working and I didn't know how to get away, you waited and—and hit me. Where's my hat?"

"We'll find your hat," Pam said. "Don't—don't get excited, Aunt Lucy."

"Why ever not?" Miss Lucinda asked. "Goodness me. Don't get excited. They tried to kill me." Then she turned her head enough to look at Barton Sandford. "I was very unjust to you, Mr. Sandford," she said. She was severe with herself. *"Very* unjust," she said. "I thought you were Doctor Crippin."

"Doctor—" he said, and Pam North said, "Oh, for heaven's sake. Cripland. And all the time it was Crippin."

"I don't—" Sandford said, his voice sounding puzzled; his expression reflecting puzzlement.

"Killed his wife," Pam North said. "Buried her—oh, in a cellar some place. Said she'd gone away. Went away himself with a girl. Got caught. Everybody knows about Doctor Crippin." She looked at Miss Lucinda, "Cripland!" she said. "How were we ever—?"

"I was wrong," Miss Lucinda said. "Paul hit me. Or the girl."

"Listen," Paul said, "did you see either of us? Just before you were hit?".

"There wasn't anybody else," Miss Lucinda said. "I suppose you say you weren't here?"

"We were here," Lynn Hickey said. "We were looking for—for some trace of Mrs. Sandford. Something that would show she had been living here. Why would we hit you? Try to kill you?" Paul looked around at the others. "Tell her, Bart," he said. "You know why we were here."

But Barton Sandford did not speak quickly. When he did, he said, "It's a funny thing about the typewriter. You say it wasn't here when you looked?"

"You heard us," Paul Logan told him.

"We all heard you, Mr. Logan," Pam North said. "I suppose what Mr. Sandford means is that you could have brought the typewriter here. To throw suspicion on Mrs. Sandford. Isn't that what you mean?" The last was to Sandford.

"Hell," Sandford said. "I don't say they did. I guess they could have. If they had—" He stopped.

"Yes," Pam said. "If they had the typewriter. But why would they have it? Your wife had it, didn't she? She wrote letters on it up to—oh, up to a few days ago."

"We didn't have it," Paul Logan said. "Mrs. North's right, of course. We—"

"Logan," Barton Sandford said, and his voice was suddenly harsh, *"what's happened to Sally?"*

"I don't know," Paul Logan said. "I thought she had—well, just gone away. As you said. But now—"

"I know what she planned," Sandford said. "What she told me she planned, there at the station in Brewster. But—I don't know what she did. She could have come back here instead. And—you stayed on for a couple of days, didn't you, Logan! At your own place? You could have—" he hesitated. "Seen that Sally did disappear."

"For God's sake," Paul Logan said. "You're crazy. Why?"

"Perhaps," Pam said, and spoke slowly, seeming to work it step by step, "perhaps she did come back here, and you saw her. Perhaps she told you she'd told her husband she was going to leave, and didn't know where she'd be. But perhaps she said she had changed her mind, and was going back to Mr. Sandford. Perhaps—isn't this what you meant, Mr. Sandford?— you and Lynn had planned to kill your mother, for the money and—and other things. You thought it would be fine to have Sally for a scapegoat; you thought it would work if it appeared she only pretended to go away, but actually had stayed here all the time. So you—saw that she did. Is that what you mean, Mr. Sandford?"

"Hell," the tall man said, his widely spaced eyes troubled. "I hadn't worked it out. I can't believe Paul would—"

"You're damned right," Paul Logan said. "You're all crazy."

"But then," Pam North said, "why did you try to kill Aunt Lucy?"

She looked down at Aunt Lucy, whose eyes now were bright.

"Make him tell you, Pamela," Miss Lucinda said.

"Listen," Dorian Weigand said, and spoke rapidly, so that they would. "We don't know any of this. Not even that Mr. Logan did hit Miss Whitsett. He's right about that; she didn't see him, or Miss Hickey. We don't know anything has happened to Mrs. Sandford. Isn't it still more likely that—well, that she was here, has been hiding here, thought Miss Whitsett had seen her and hit her so that she would have time to get away? That now she's hiding some other place?"

It was a damn sight more likely, Paul Logan said. At least one of them had some sense.

"Oh," Pam said. "Several, really. The thing to do is to find her, isn't it? If she's alive, of course, but even if not. Don't you think so too, Mr. Sandford?"

"I told you—" Sandford began, but little Miss Lucinda interrupted him.

"But she isn't, dear," Miss Lucinda said. "I looked everywhere, even down in that dreadful cellar. There wasn't a place in the cement. I was down there when Mr. Logan and Miss Hickey were here, you know, and that was the reason I couldn't catch up with them." She looked at Paul Logan. "Or thought I couldn't," she said. "And with the telephone off and everything—"

She stopped.

"What is it, dear?" she said to Pam North, who was looking at her, or through her. "You look so—so thoughtful, Pamela."

"The telephone's been turned off," Pam said, slowly and carefully. "But the electricity is still on. Isn't that rather unusual, Mr. Sandford? I'd think if one, why not the other?"

"My goodness," Miss Lucinda said. "Goodness me. The little wheel was turning, wasn't it? But there weren't any lights on. How—how very *unobservant* of me." She started to sit up; perhaps the movement brought pain to her head; perhaps it was because of that that she paled. "But how horrible," she said. "How really horrible." She closed her eyes. "So cold," she said, and shivered, half a dozen feet from the leaping fire.

"Probably," the man next the driver said, "we'll be late for the party. Probably it's all loused."

"You worry too much, Saul," one of the men in the back seat told him. "You can't hurry Washington by worrying."

"Clearance," Saul said. "Always clearance. Through channels. It might as well be the damned army. So everybody gets there first. Louses the whole thing up."

"They're talking about murder," the second man in the back seat said, quietly. "Makes them hurry, I shouldn't wonder."

"Damn it," Saul said, "he's our man. They were as good as told that."

The car merely hooted at the Brewster light; the driver did not hesitate. He knew the way. He went on the way at seventy.

" 'Murder comes first,' this inspector of theirs kept saying," the second man in the rear seat said. "It will, you know."

"And we pick up the pieces," Saul said. "If we hadn't had to clear with so damned many. It was

London did it. They must have been asleep in London."

Very probably they had been, the second man in the rear admitted. It was a not unreasonable hour to be asleep in London.

"So we hold the bag," Saul said.

The car slowed abruptly; swung left off the highway

"Maybe he'll figure an out," the second man in the rear said, after he had regained his balance.

11

It wasn't, Barton Sandford said, at all unusual to leave electric power on in a summer cottage, even when the telephone was discontinued for the winter. Now and then, in late fall, even on mild days in the winter, they wanted to get out of town and come to the cottage and then needed electricity, but could do without a telephone. And they usually left a few things in the deep freeze, to have them handy. They'd got a big deep freezer that summer to—

And then he stopped; then his eyes widened and his face set; then, in an odd voice, he said, "My God!"

The five of them crowded the kitchen; Miss Lucinda, her eyes closed, sat by the fire. "So silly of me to make that mistake," Miss Lucinda said to herself. "Cripland indeed."

There was a shining padlock on the deep freezer. Sandford and Logan, Lynn and Pam and Dorian stopped in front of it; looked at it. It seemed to Pam very cold here in the kitchen, away from the fire.

"All right," Sandford said. He selected a key from a chain of keys and opened the lock. He reached out. "There's no use—"

He lifted the top of the big freezer, and for a moment seemed unable to look down into it. Then he did look.

And then, in a suddenly flat voice, he said that he'd be damned.

"My God," he said, "you really had me going there for a minute." He turned to Pam North. "Look yourself," he said. "You and that aunt of yours!"

It was obvious that there was no point in looking; everything in Barton Sandford's attitude told them that. But, during the few seconds after the idea had, it seemed, come to all of them at once—come when Pam talked of electricity, Aunt Lucinda became so suddenly cold—a vision had grown so uglily clear in Pam North's mind that even the fact could not quite destroy it. The fact was that the freezer was empty; completely empty. It was a bitterly, needlessly, cold and empty shell. In it were not even the things one might expect to find in a freezer. Barton Sandford let the lid drop.

"I tell you," he said to all of them, "we're crazy. She's gone. She's been here and left the typewriter, but now she's gone again."

At first his voice had seemed to hold relief; as he continued, it grew more puzzled.

"Damn it," he said, "I'm afraid—"

"Goodness me," Miss Lucinda said, from the kitchen door. "I thought you understood. Not there now, of course. The closet—where I was." She hesitated. "That," she said, and now she swayed a little, and held to the door jamb for support—"that's why it was so cold in there, I'm afraid."

It was Sandford who reached the closet door first this time, not Paul Logan. It was he who pushed aside the hanging, concealing clothes.

The body of a young woman, unclothed, knees doubled up to chin, was at the end of the closet, fitted between its walls. It was, indeed, very cold in the closet, and the coldness was more—far more—than that of death.

Wordlessly, Barton Sandford turned. At first there seemed to be no expression in his eyes; then his pleasant face contorted; then, with his hands out, clutching, he moved toward Paul Logan. And the slight, handsome young man drew back; drew back warily.

"No," he said. "You're crazy, Bart. I didn't—"

"Paul!" Lynn Hickey said. *"Paul! He's—"*

"Stand still, Mr. Sandford," Dorian Weigand said. "Don't do anything."

Her voice was quiet in the room—quiet and decisive. And she had in her hand what must, surely, have been one of the smallest automatic pistols ever made. But it looked big enough.

"Why!" Pam North said. "Why! Dorian Weigand!"

"Bill's idea," Dorian said. "Stand still, Mr. Sandford. That isn't the way." Mr. Sandford stood still. "Since I got kidnaped," Dorian said. "Of course, not always." She did not take her eyes from Sandford. "Only when I'm with you, dear," she said to Pamela North.

"Well," Pam said. "Of all things." She looked into the closet. "Of all dreadful things," she said, in a different voice. "All horrible things."

"All right," Barton Sandford said. "I won't—it's all right, now." His voice was steady, hard. "You killed her," he told Paul Logan. "By God, I didn't believe it. When—when I was saying it, I didn't believe it."

"I didn't kill her," Paul Logan said. "You ought to know that. Because the only possible reason—a made-up reason—would be that I—I killed mother."

"You must have done that too," Sandford said, and spoke slowly. "Tried to lay it on Sally. Killed Sally first—so you could. Used her key to—to—the freezer—" He paused and shook his head. "Such a damned hideous thing," he said.

"Yes," Pamela North said. "It is hideous. Why, Mr. Sandford?"

He looked at her. Momentarily he appeared puzzled.

"Ask him," he said, and gestured toward Paul Logan.

"Not me," Logan said.

"Oh surely," Pam said. "One of you can think. Someone—your wife, Mr. Sandford—is killed oh—almost six weeks ago. And—and frozen. Because—I'm sure you can think of the reason, Mr. Sandford."

Dorian still held the little automatic. But she looked at Pam North, and her expression was more puzzled than Sandford's had been.

"Please," Pam North said, "just keep it pointed, Dorian. So—so if anybody tries—"

"What the hell?" Sandford said. "I've said I won't hurt the little—won't hurt Logan."

"You see," Pam said, "six weeks is a long time. But with—with the body frozen, there wouldn't be any change, would there? Or—not much, anyway. So that, if Mrs. Sandford had been found a few hours from now, after she—after the body wasn't frozen any more—anyone might think she'd just died, mightn't they? That she had been alive when Mrs. Logan was killed; perhaps even been alive a few hours ago, when Aunt Lucy was hit—that she'd killed Aunt Lucy, because the poor little thing would have been dead then, and then herself. If—if there'd been a few hours. If Dorian and I hadn't come—what would you say, Mr. Sandford—barging in?"

"My God, Logan!" Barton Sandford said. "Was that the—?"

"No," Pam North said. "Oh no, Mr. Sandford. Not Mr. Logan, of course. You—Mr. Sandford. You can give the other up, now, because—*Dorian!*"

But the warning was late, too late. By then, moving with sudden violence, Sandford had the little automatic. He held it, backing clear so that he could point it as he chose.

"We've had enough of this," Sandford said. "More than enough. We'll call it off, now."

"Damn," said Dorian Weigand.

"It's no use, Mr. Sandford," Pam said. "You'll never get away."

"Get away?" Barton Sandford said. "I'm not going to get away. I'm going to turn Logan in. Because you see, Mrs. North, you're all wrong about it. Maybe part of your story's right, but the man's wrong. I—"

But he stopped, because Pam was shaking her head slowly, with finality.

"I tell you it's no use," she said. "I've known—oh, for hours. Because of the telephone, you know."

He looked at her. He said he didn't get it. His eyes flickered to the telephone on the table between the beds.

"Not that one," Pam said. "Ours. The one you called me on yesterday, to invite me to lunch. You see, Mr. Sandford, you shouldn't have known the number, should you? Because it's not listed. But you did know it and it was written down in Aunt Thelma's room at the hotel. She'd written, 'Pamela,' and then the number. You got it when you went to put the poison in her suitcase, of course."

"Somebody—" Sandford began, but again Pam shook her head.

"I don't think so," she said. "Of course, if you could prove it—prove that Jerry gave it to you, or Bill Weigand or—any of the people who know it. But—you can't, can you Mr. Sandford? Because nobody will lie for you, now, will they?" She looked toward the closet. "Maybe you killed the only person who would lie for you," she said.

"Sally!" Sandford said, and there was no simulation, now, of the surprise in his tone. "Not that one. She'd see me in—"

And then he stopped.

"You know—" he began.

Paul Logan jumped him, then. He jumped recklessly, straight at the man who towered over him. Barton Sandford did not use the little gun to stop him.

He used his fist, hard, catching the slight, leaping boy in the throat. Logan staggered back.

"—too damn much," Sandford told Pam North, and had her by the wrist, bending her arm behind her, pressing the little automatic against her body.

Pam said, "Ow-w!" and twisted, kicking. But the pain in her arm increased and she was quiet, white-faced. She said, "Won't do you any good," and Sandford pulled her, by the twisted arm, close against him. Paul Logan, whiter than Pam, gasping for breath, moved to come in again, but Sandford moved the little gun to cover him—to cover him and Dorian. It stopped them. Sandford began to back out of the room, jerking Pam with him.

"Even if you do kill me," Pam said, but the words faltered. (*Jerry! Why aren't you here, Jerry? I'm—I'm afraid!*)

Pam was told, abruptly, harshly, to shut up. The voice hardly sounded like Sandford's. It told her she talked too damn much.

In the living room, he turned them about, with her in front, and pushed her ahead, moving rapidly across the room. She didn't know what the others did; couldn't think of what they might do.

Jerry would be there, she told herself. Jerry and Bill and—and Mullins. He would open the door to push her through it and a voice would say—what would the voice say? It—this couldn't be *it!*

He reached around her and opened the door, and nobody stood in it. He pushed her through, and slammed the door behind them. He would make for one of the cars—the one he had hired; the Logan car, blocking the entrance. But he did not.

He held her differently, now. He held her wrist and pulled her behind him. He was running, not toward the cars; running in the darkness down beside the house, beyond it, following a trail with his feet in the darkness. She stumbled and almost fell, and he yanked her up and kept going.

She half ran, half fell, after him. She stepped sidewise on a stone and her ankle twisted, but he yanked
her up again before she struck the ground. They
seemed to be going down hill, as a road had gone once,
long ago—a road now only faint openness among
trees, a just distinguishable lessening of roughness
under foot.

"Stop!" Pam tried to say. "You can't—" But there
was no breath for words; the sounds she made were
hardly words. She was told, again, to shut up; he
wrenched again at the arm he held, and pain shot into
her shoulder. She'd fall, finally—she'd fall—he would
have to drag her—she did fall, but again he held her
from the ground.

"Stand up!" he said, and called her names. "Stand
up, you—"

She could not tell how far they had come, how far he
had dragged her through the night along the faintness
of the trail; she could see almost nothing, even as her
eyes grew accustomed to darkness—only the big man
in front of her; only that, the way they were going,
there was a difference in the darkness. That was
because—oh yes, the road had been cleared through
trees; the greater darkness on either side was the
darkness of the trees. They fled down a dark corridor
in darkness. It would go on and on and—

He stopped, pulled her again against him. At their
right was—something. Then he had got a match from
somewhere—no, a cigarette lighter—and the tiny light
reflected from metal. A car, backed off at right angles
to the trail—hidden there—

"Your car," she said. "The one your wife was
supposed—"

"I told you to shut up," he said, and slapped her
across the mouth with an open hand. "Shut up."

He dragged her around the car; low bushes tore at
their clothing, fought to keep them from the car. A
whiplike branch, pushed back by him and then re-

leased, stung across her face. Then they were beyond the right hand door of the car, and he was opening it, forcing her in. He pushed her under the wheel.

"Get it started," he told her. "Cut sharp right as you come out. Use the low lights."

She hesitated. He thrust the little gun against her side, bored it into her side. He said, "Get going."

She switched on the lights, threw the beam down as he directed; started the motor.

"Cut it sharp," he said. "Take it slow."

"There's—there's no road," she said, and was told there was road enough. The lights showed there was— just enough. "Stay on it," he told her. "Be damned sure." He dug the little gun harder into her side.

She let the clutch in, cutting hard to the right; letting the clutch slip as the car moved slowly out of the bushes, turned slowly onto the tracks which had to do for road. She stayed in low, let the car creep along the tracks. It was better not to die here—better to keep alive a little—

Then the pressure of the gun against her was suddenly relaxed and the màn beside her made an odd sound—a wordless sound, hardly more than an in-drawn breath.

"All right, stop it now," a voice said. "We're not going any place."

He had changed his—*no, it was another voice*.

She stopped the car.

"That's right," the new voice said. A light came on behind them; the beam from a big flashlight. "Sit still," the new man said, and then the light moved as he, himself, got out of the back seat in which—in which, of course, he had hidden to wait for them. He was beside the car, now the beam full on them. "If you've got a gun, Sandford, I'd drop it," the new man said. He had an automatic of his own; a much larger automatic. Sandford dropped the little gun.

"Get out, now," the man said. Then, unexpectedly,

he whistled shrilly. "Get around in front where we can have a look at you."

Sandford got out. The man kept the light on him. "Come on," he said to Pam. "You too." She slid across the seat. *Oh, they'd come! After all, they'd been in time!* But—who were they?

She followed Sandford into the area illuminated by the car's headlights.

"Well," said the medium man—the man who had followed her up Fifth Avenue and back again, and into Saks. "Well, look who's here. So—I was right that time, wasn't I? All right, both you, get your hands where I can see them. Out in front of you, say."

"But I—" Pam said. "You don't want *me!*"

"Now sister," the medium man said. "Now sister. Why ever not?"

"Because I'm—" Pam began and stopped. "He was—was making me come along. As a—a hostage or something."

"Well now, think of that," the medium man said, in his rather pleasant voice. "Just think of that, sister. Shows how wrong a guy can be, doesn't it?"

She looked up at him, her eyes wide.

"Because," he said, "I'd figure you were in it with him. Up to your pretty neck, sister." He motioned. "Right up to here," he said, and cut with the barrel of the automatic, quickly, across his own throat. Then he pointed the pistol again at them. Then he whistled again.

"O.K.," a voice shouted from the direction of the cottage. "Got 'em?"

The medium man yelled back. He yelled, "Got 'em."

"O.K.," the distant voice said. "Bring 'em along up."

They left the car, its lights still burning, and worked around it, Sandford first, Pam after him, the man with the gun and the light behind them. They went back the way Sandford had run, with Pam dragging behind him. With each step, Pam's twisted ankle was pierced by pain. Seeing her limp, the medium man moved up to her, half supported her.

They came around the cottage, came to the front door, which was open, with light coming out of it, with a man standing just outside. The man said, "Hello, Sandford. Think you were going somewhere?"

Sandford merely swore.

"Tut tut," the man said. "Ladies, Sandford. You're pretty little—" He looked at Pam. "My, my," he said, "what did you run into, sister?"

Pam North pointed at Sandford.

"He," she said. "He—slapped me." Then she realized she was crying. "And he killed his wife."

"Baby wants to sing, Saul," the medium man said. "Boy, does baby want to sing."

"That's nice," Saul said. "That's very nice. Take them along in. We've got quite a little nest of them in here." His voice hardened. "Quite a nice little nest of lousy spies. Take them along—"

But then he stopped. A car, its headlights blazing, stopped half off the road, blocked by the Logan car. Almost before it stopped, three men were out of it, running toward the house. Saul's hands streaked under his coat and the automatic in the hand of the medium man leaped up.

"*Jerry!*" Pam screamed. "*Jerry! Look out. They're*—"

The medium man fired and Pam screamed again.

"Saul!" Bill Weigand yelled, and stopped. "Tell your damned G-boy to—"

"Hold it," Saul said to the medium man, the words snapping. "You're a lousy shot. Look who's here," he said to Bill Weigand—to Jerry, to Sergeant Mullins. "You boys are right late for school."

Jerry kept on coming. He had Pam North in his arms. She clung to him, crying.

"Jerry," she said. "Jerry—they think I'm a *spy!*"

"My God," Jerry said, holding onto her tightly. "The things you get into! Listen, Pam—"

But then he said nothing, but only held her close and let her cry.

"I tell you," the medium man said, apparently to Saul. "She was a contact. I figured all along she—"

"It looks," Saul said, mildly, "as if a lot of people have been figuring." He looked at Bill Weigand. "Thought you'd get here first," he said.

Bill looked at Mullins. He looked at Mullins sadly.

"O.K., Loot," Mullins said. "I got us lost." He looked at Pamela North, in her husband's arms; he looked at her thoughtfully, as if about to make some rather prodigious comment. But then he said only, "It's sort of confusing in the country, Loot."

"Right," Bill Weigand said. He also looked at Pam. He said, "Pam, Dorian—"

Pam nodded her head vigorously. She spoke in a tearful voice, further muffled by Jerry's coat sleeve.

"—s'all right," she said. "Only—only they probably think she's a spy too." Then, suddenly, she freed herself. She looked at Sandford.

"You mean," she said, "he's a spy? As well as a murderer?" Nobody answered immediately. "Goodness," Pamela North said. "And until just a few hours ago, I thought he worked for the government." She looked at Sandford further. "I guess," she said, "because his eyes are so wide apart." She turned to Bill. "I still don't understand most of it," she said. "About the telephone and the deep freeze, yes. But—what was it all about?"

"Deep freeze?" Bill Weigand said. "I—" Then he interrupted himself. "Barton Sandford," he said, "I arrest you on a charge of—"

"Hey," Saul said, "wait a minute!"

"—homicide," Bill Weigand finished, and then smiled pleasantly at Saul.

"Mean you hadn't got around to it?" he asked Saul

pleasantly. "Well, wouldn't have mattered much anyway, would it? Because, as the inspector says, murder comes first."

"You mean," Pam North said, *"our* inspector said that? *Arty?"* Bill Weigand nodded. "Goodness," Pam said. "Goodness me."

12

Martini sat on Miss Thelma Whitsett's lap, for reasons explicable only to Martini. It was her custom to sit much on Pam North's lap; often, although less often, on Jerry's. The laps of other humans commonly did not, to Martini, exist; other humans were, at best, to be tolerated if they kept their proper place. But now she sat on Miss Thelma Whitsett's lap, although Miss Whitsett did not greatly want her there. Miss Thelma Whitsett, who did not at all care for cats, sat rigid. She was aware, having been told, that the presence on her of this blue-eyed cat was a compliment; she wished it were a compliment bestowed elsewhere. Without appearing to, she had, a few minutes before, gently pushed at Martini. Martini had turned her head and presented very sharp and white teeth for inspection. Martini had not said anything, or otherwise done anything, but Miss Thelma had decided not to press the matter.

"The idea," Pam North said, "of thinking *I'm* a spy. The very idea!"

"Nobody does now, dear," Miss Lucinda Whitsett said. She was in the same black silk dress, or one identical. She was not wearing the pink hat, or any hat. She was wearing a bandage, less spectacular and, on

198

the whole, rather more becoming. "The moving finger writes and having writ—"

She paused of her own accord and looked at her sister Thelma. Thelma's lips parted slightly, but she did not speak.

"—moves on," Miss Lucinda said. "This too shall, I mean has, passed."

Miss Pennina Whitsett finished her small glass of sherry, shook her head at Jerry North, and accepted a canapé. She noted that all was well that ended well.

Miss Thelma made a slight movement, inadvertently touching Martini. Martini turned, looked at her darkly and said "O-w-w!" in a guttural voice. Miss Thelma, moving cautiously, sipped from her own glass of sherry. Martini turned away and put her chin thoughtfully on a paw curled to receive it. She partially closed her eyes and looked at Pam North, who had a small adhesive bandage on her upper lip and a scratch, outlined in iodine, on her forehead.

"I do wish," Miss Lucinda said, "that we knew *all* about it. Goodness. Leaving in the morning for Florida and not ever knowing! Goodness me."

They knew, Pam pointed out, that Barton Sandford had killed his wife, apparently also with cyanide, and put her body in a deep freezer for preservation. They knew, or were at least certain, that he had killed Grace Logan.

"But not why," Jerry pointed out, going to mix martinis for himself and Pam. "Or do we?"

"Because she found out about Mrs. Sandford," Pam said. "At least, I guess so. And that he was some sort of spy or something like that; that the FBI was after him, not part of him. I mean, not he of it. We know he hit Aunt Lucy, or I guess we do."

"Goodness," Aunt Lucinda said. "Whatever happened to my hat?"

It had been, Pam told her gently, badly damaged. It had been, shapelessly pink, in a corner of the closet in which Aunt Lucinda had been. Probably, it still was. She did not think even Aunt Lucinda had remembered it.

"I fainted," Miss Lucinda pointed out. "How could I? Really, Pamela, it was—" She stopped. "But it's not your fault, dear," she said. "You must have had so many things on your mind. That awful man. I can always get another hat."

Not, Jerry thought, twisting lemon peel over martinis, another hat like that one. It did not stand to reason. He made no remark, however.

"Speaking of hats," Pam said, "did you just pull Doctor Crippin out of one? I mean, there wasn't anything else?"

"Of course not, dear," Miss Lucinda said. "I just said to myself, now what is this like? And then, of course, I thought of Mr. Cripland—I mean Crippin. So I was sure the body must be there and I went to look." She smiled at Pamela gently. "It was perfectly simple, dear," she said. "Once you thought of it."

Pamela North ran the fingers of her right hand gently through her hair. Although it was a gesture rare with her, it had a curious kind of familiarity. She looked across the room toward Jerry, who was coming with cocktails.

"Oh," Pam North said.

"Perfectly simple, Pam," Jerry said, his voice grave. "Surely you see that?"

"I—" Pam said, and swallowed. "Is Bill really coming? It's all so—so unsatisfactory."

Bill Weigand was coming if he could make it, Jerry said, telling Pam gently what she already knew, handing her a glass. He hoped with Dorian; in any case, he had two more cocktail glasses chilling.

"Of course, Pamela," Aunt Thelma said, looking rather pointedly at the new glass, "it isn't any of my business but—"

The movement occasioned by speech was transmitted to Miss Thelma's lap. Martini almost audibly sighed. Then she turned her head, laid back her pointed ears, and bit the nearer of Miss Thelma's hands. She did not bite to hurt, or even to puncture. She bit to show she could. She then left Miss Thelma's lap, and the room.

"Well," Miss Thelma said. "Of all things!"

"I always feel," Miss Pennina Whitsett said, apparently to the canapé in her hand, "that one should not be critical."

"Well," Miss Thelma said, "of all things, Pennina."

"I—" Pam said, quickly. But then the doorbell rang, in a special rhythm. Jerry let Bill Weigand in. Dorian was with him. Gin and Sherry, the former chasing the latter, came to help receive. Sherry stood on hind legs, put her forepaws against Dorian's knee, and—from the sound—wept bitterly.

"Hello, Sherry," Dorian said. "Hello, Gin." She looked around. "Hello, Martini, wherever you are," she said, politely. Then she said, "Pam, I'm sorry about the gun. It was very embarrassing. Bill was quite disappointed in me."

Bill Weigand grinned at her; he grinned tiredly. Jerry made more drinks while the aunts greeted and were greeted in return. Bill, sitting, drank half of his cocktail rapidly and said, "Um-m-m!" He took another sip. The others looked at him.

"Mr. Sandford is not coöperative," Bill told them, and finished his drink. "Keeps saying we're crazy; why don't we get on to Paul Logan; keeps on running a bluff. So—we'll have to prove it." He looked at Miss Lucinda Whitsett. They would, he told her, have to ask her to come back for the trial.

"Oh goodness," Miss Lucinda said. "Oh goodness me." But her voice was extremely cheerful. "Whatever for? Surely not just because he's Doctor Crippin?"

"Crippin?" Bill repeated. His face cleared. "Oh

yes," he said. "Well, no, Miss Whitsett. To testify you looked in the closet thoroughly. You did, didn't you? Before anybody else came?"

"Oh yes," Miss Lucinda said. "I did look. The—I suppose that's what you mean?—the—it wasn't there."

"Right," Bill said. "I know it wasn't. Not until Sandford put it there. About the telephone, Pam— you'll have to testify too. It will help. We—we may need everything. For the murders, that is. The other'll be easier. Saul keeps pointing that out; telling everybody they ought to have him first. They won't; nor second either, I hope."

"Bill," Pam said, "could we begin earlier? Nearer the beginning. Where is he now?"

That, Bill Weigand told her, was the ending, not the beginning. He was in the Putnam County jail in Carmel. He had been, since the night before, under interrogation by the State Police, the Putnam County District Attorney, the New York City police—represented by Weigand and Mullins—Thompkins from the New York County District Attorney's office, and three men from the Federal Bureau of Investigation. He was being very stubborn. But—there would be points, of course. There always were, confession or no confession. Little things that didn't fit.

"For instance," Bill said, "he says now that, to his knowledge, Mrs. Logan had not been in his apartment since Sally's disappearance. But, when I talked to him first, he said she had. So—we've got hold of the woman who came to clean the apartment, since we knew what to look for, and she says she let Mrs. Logan in once and that she waited there half an hour or so before Sandford got home."

"I don't—" Pam said, puzzled.

"Mrs. Logan saw the typewriter," Bill told her. "We can't prove it; he won't admit it. We can prove she might have; we can show that, if she did, he had a reasonable motive to kill her. Assuming, of course, that this is the one they decide to try first. They may stick to the other. I'd think they probably would."

"Please," Pam said. "Can't you begin earlier?"

He could with another drink, Bill indicated. He was given another drink.

He couldn't tell them, he said, after sipping, lighting a cigarette, precisely when it did begin—months before, certainly; perhaps a year or so before. It had begun when Barton Sandford, not for principles but for money, began to act as a go-between in some sort of espionage mechanism. How that happened, Bill Weigand didn't know; where exactly Sandford had stood in the organization, Bill also didn't know. He assumed, somewhere between rather pathetic amateurs at the bottom and not at all pathetic professionals at the top. He assumed that atomic secrets did not enter into it; what did, he told them he couldn't say. But Sandford was, authentically, a biochemist, for whatever that might indicate.

"You really don't know, Bill?" Dorian asked from the chair in which she was curled, with Sherry curled on her. Bill smiled quickly, perhaps slightly shook his head. They could take it he didn't know; that the government boys were very secretive. "And if you did, it wouldn't make any difference," Dorian told him, and to this Bill said, "Right, darling." Then he went on.

How Sally Sandford had become suspicious of her husband's activities, nobody knew, or was likely to. Perhaps something had happened at Gimo's, which seemed to be a meeting place. (It was because it was a meeting place that the agent Bill knew had been there Monday night.) Perhaps something had happened at the country cottage; Sandford had also met contacts there, at least later, when he was under surveillance. At any rate, she did get suspicious. Apparently, she had told her husband of her suspicions. What happened then between them could only be guessed, since she was dead and he was not cooperating. It was a safe bet that she had threatened to turn him in.

"A righteous person," Pam said. "Sacrificing one for many. Paul Logan said that."

Bill Weigand supposed so. At any rate, she had turned him in.

"But—" Pam said.

Bill shrugged. He admitted the alternatives. Either Sandford, knowing she had reported him, had killed her vengefully or, possibly, to prevent her telling more. Or, which seemed to him more probable, she had—playing, as she thought, for safety—pretended to be argued out of her intention, while secretly instrumenting it, expecting the FBI to take action which would protect her. She may so have convinced her husband she had not reported him, but not that she did not plan to. He thought he had killed in time.

"I suspect that," Bill said, "because they say he gave no indication he suspected he was under observation until after Mrs. Logan was killed, which was when he found out he was being followed. Probably, until then, he thought he was in the clear as long as the murder wasn't discovered. It must have been—quite a shock, since it meant he'd killed twice to no purpose."

"Locked the barn door after the horse," Aunt Lucinda said, clarifyingly.

That was, Bill agreed—and finished his cocktail—what it came to. He had killed once to keep a secret which was no longer a secret, and the second time because he had slipped up on the first murder. His plan had been not unreasonable; it might have worked. It had been to keep his wife apparently alive long after she was dead—and to keep her body frozen so that the actual time of death would be impossible to determine accurately. Undoubtedly he had planned, at his convenience, to remove the body from the freezer, dress it, put cyanide and a glass of water beside it. The body would have taken many hours to—well, to thaw. Meanwhile, he would establish an alibi which could not be broken. Then, he would arrange to find his wife's body, or have it found—probably the latter. And death would appear to have occurred within a matter of a few hours—the hours for which he was covered.

"Goodness me," Aunt Lucinda said. "What an unpleasant mind Mr. Sandford has."

"Would it have worked?" Pam asked.

One couldn't be sure, Bill told her. But—probably it would. In the city—well, in the city you would have run up against the best experts. Outside the city—probably it would have worked. Probably it would have worked anywhere for a jury, which was what one came to in the end, whatever experts might suspect.

It had not come to that because, waiting in Sandford's apartment to talk to him about Sally, Mrs. Logan had accidentally found the typewriter—the typewriter she knew to be Sally's, the one on which Sally apparently was writing her letters from the middle west—letters Sandford had flown back and forth to mail. The FBI would prove the trips; it, also, had made them.

"The right typewriter," Pam said. "In the wrong place." She considered. "Like my mind was, most of the time," she said. "I thought the wrong typewriter, that he was FBI—and that Sally killed her aunt."

"Right," Bill said. "The last, anyway, you were supposed to think—or consider a possibility. After involving Miss Whitsett didn't work."

There, it was evident, Sandford had improvised. The Misses Whitsett had seemed a gift; Miss Thelma Whitsett was suspected. It was a convenience. He had, by going to the hotel—finding them absent (he would have made some excuse had they been in their rooms), planting the poison, he had endeavored to enhance suspicion. It had not been well thought out, but it involved little risk.

"Until he used the telephone number," Pam pointed out.

"Right," Bill said. "I suppose the fact that the telephone might not be listed never occurred to him. He wanted to see you to pump you, of course—and to make a good impression, get you on his side. Knowing about you, Pam, he figured that would be a good idea."

"It almost was," Pam agreed.

After her luncheon with Sandford, Pam had been followed by the FBI man—the "medium" man—as a matter of routine. All of Sandford's associates were being checked; the FBI was far from ready to move in.

"I was a bird of feather, flocking," Pam said. "But it came out all right." She regarded the dress she was wearing. "Nice new feathers," she observed, and stroked the dress with affection. Jerry North went to mix more drinks.

Aside from what the government could prove against Sandford, which probably was plenty, evidence against Sandford was, and probably would remain, fairly circumstantial, Bill Weigand said. The presence of the typewriter in his apartment, which the maid would swear to—that was a fact. His telephone call to Pam North—that was a fact. And it was a fact, almost flatly provable, that he had removed his wife's body from the freezer, planning to set the stage for the suicide tableau, being interrupted by the arrival of Pam and Dorian. (He would have, Bill pointed out, seen their approaching lights in time to push the body into the closet, having already removed it to the bedroom.)

He was the only person who could have done it. Three people, one of them—Miss Lucinda—immaculately disinterested, could testify that, before Miss Lucinda was struck, the body had not been in the closet and the typewriter, apparently, not in the house. And another person was involved—the man who had been following Sandford.

"Oh!" Pam said. "Then all the time—"

"Right," Bill said. "All the time. But he was under orders to wait for the rest before moving in. Anyway—"

Anyway, the agent who was following had left his car some distance down the approach road to the cottage and walked—apparently half run—the rest of the way. He had got in front of the cottage in time to be passed by a couple he now knew were Paul Logan and Lynn Hickey. He had avoided being seen; come from a shadow in time to see Sandford with somebody just outside the door. It was too dark to get details; the shadows of Sandford and his companion were almost one. But there could be no doubt that it was Sandford, carrying Miss Lucinda in. It took Logan and the girl out of it; so validated their testimony. It also proved, of course, that Sandford had been in the cottage for upward of an hour when Pam and Dorian arrived, not the few minutes he pretended. He had had time enough to get the stage partly set.

"But the audience came early," Dorian said. "Before curtain time."

That was it, of course, Bill agreed. Presumably, Miss Lucinda was to be found dead, presumptively the victim of Sally who then, with things closing in on her, had killed herself.

"Of course," Bill Weigand said abstractedly, looking at Miss Lucinda Whitsett, "he wouldn't have killed you until the body thawed."

"Mercy," Miss Lucinda said. "It's all rather like a story I read about a young couple on a glacier in the Alps and—"

"*Lucinda!*" Aunt Thelma said.

There was a momentary pause.

"Thelma, dear," Miss Lucinda said then. "I've been meaning to say something for years. I do wish you wouldn't use that tone." She smiled. "Not to me, anyway," she said. "Not to dear Pennina, either. It's so—why, it's almost censorious, Thelma. It would be so easy for people to misunderstand you, dear."

And then Miss Lucinda arose. Perhaps because her head still hurt a little, she swayed slightly. Perhaps it was because the air she breathed had become, suddenly, strangely rarified.

"I'm afraid we must go now, Pamela," she said. "It's been so interesting."

They went. Miss Lucinda Whitsett led the way.

Pam and Jerry, Bill and Dorian, looked after them.

"I do wish," Dorian said, "that I'd ever got to see that hat. It must have been—" She paused.

"It was," Pam North said. "It certainly *was!*"